SPECIAL MESSAGE TO READERS

THE ULVERSCROFT FOUNDATION
(registered UK charity number 264873)
was established in 1972 to provide funds for research, diagnosis and treatment of eye diseases. Examples of major projects funded by the Ulverscroft Foundation are:

- The Children's Eye Unit at Moorfields Eye Hospital, London
- The Ulverscroft Children's Eye Unit at Great Ormond Street Hospital for Sick Children
- Funding research into eye diseases and treatment at the Department of Ophthalmology, University of Leicester
- The Ulverscroft Vision Research Group, Institute of Child Health
- Twin operating theatres at the Western Ophthalmic Hospital, London
- The Chair of Ophthalmology at the Royal Australian College of Ophthalmologists

You can help further the work of the Foundation by making a donation or leaving a legacy. Every contribution is gratefully received. If you would like to help support the Foundation or require further information, please contact:

THE ULVERSCROFT FOUNDATION
The Green, Bradgate Road, Anstey
Leicester LE7 7FU, England
Tel: (0116) 236 4325
website: www.ulverscroft-foundation.org.uk

GREENVILLE RAIDERS

While Sheriff Flint is out of town, bandits strike Greenville Bank. Only they have come at the wrong time and do not get the haul they expected, instead leaving behind a trail of destruction.

On Flint's return, he is faced with a deadly situation. When a beautiful woman and her elderly father get involved, Flint thinks at first that they are a liability, especially when he discovers that he has to lead a posse into the dangerous borderlands between Greenville and Mexico. And then his brave deputy is embroiled in a fight to save a gold consignment on its way to town . . .

ALEX FREW

GREENVILLE RAIDERS

Complete and Unabridged

LINFORD
Leicester

First published in Great Britain in 2020 by
Robert Hale
an imprint of The Crowood Press
Wiltshire

First Linford Edition
published 2023
by arrangement with The Crowood Press
Wiltshire

A catalogue record for this book is available from the British Library.

ISBN 978–1–4448–5022–2

Published by
Ulverscroft Limited
Anstey, Leicestershire

Printed and bound in Great Britain by
TJ Books Ltd., Padstow, Cornwall

This book is printed on acid-free paper

To my parents Alex senior and Isabelle,
who gave me everything I needed to
become a writer.

1

Horses' hoofs pounded on the ground of the town as the riders came into Greenville, a settlement in Dona Ana County in New Mexico. The town was just across from the Mexican border, and many of the inhabitants of Greenville were of Mexican extraction. Indeed the alternative name for the town was 'La Verde', since many of those who lived there did not speak English.

Riders coming into town were not unusual, because of where Greenville was located: the borders were places where people were always coming and going. But these intruders were different in that all four men were riding fast and sure, wearing bandannas of various hues tied around their faces. Neither did they waste much time as they headed straight past the saloon — the destination for most travellers — although not usually at this early hour, because it was barely nine in the morning. Neither did any of the men waste time on their trip. They headed straight for a building marked with a painted banner on the side that said 'Greenville Bank and Loan', a sure sign that the area had some economic success.

The four men dismounted briskly, and tied the reins of their horses loosely around the hitching post outside the bank. Three of them walked inside, leaving one in the open who stood with his hand at his hip, clutching the butt of his gun but hiding it well from the sight of any members of the public with the flaps of his long, black cotton coat.

The bank wasn't large, but there was a wide space between the entrance and the counter, at which sat only one clerk. The counter reached from floor to ceiling and was finished in planed wood that had been stained a dark brown. This early, they had no customers.

Those who had gone into the building did not waste any time. Only one of them spoke. He was wearing a long brown coat, and carried a pistol in each hand. His voice was harsh, but he spoke clearly, and in English.

'Don't waste any time here, I want the gold shipment, and I want it now.'

Three bank clerks were present, the one at the counter and the other two who were working on ledgers at a large square table behind him, who had stopped work as soon as the raiders appeared.

One of the clerks got to his feet and pushed away the smaller one sitting at the counter. He was a big man with a fairly muscular frame, this showing as he easily overthrew the other man, and his thatch of brown hair flopped across his brow as he thrust out his square jaw and glared at the three invaders. His voice was just as harsh as that of the man who had given them their orders.

'Get out of here you idjits, the gold was supposed to be here but it never came — there was a delay.'

The equally large criminal who had made the demand seemed to be puzzled by this information.

'You're lying,' he said. 'That can't be true.'

'You boys have made a terrible mistake, now git out of here, or you'll have made the biggest blunder of your lives.'

One of the crooks raised a pistol in his hand and aimed it at the big man. The gunman was clearly not about to take the answer as verbatim.

'The gold, take us to it right now, or you die.' He spoke with a harsh Mexican accent. He was clearly just one second away from calling the other man 'gringo'.

'Hey,' the clerk looked at the leader of the robbers. 'I'm not lying, believe me, bud!' There was an imperceptible pause, and the largest of the robbers turned to his men.

'Come away from here boys, because there's no point if . . .' but he was too late, because the Mexican who had spoken had raised his gun and fired at the large clerk. The man tried to throw his body away from the shot, and he was helped by the leader of the bandits, who managed to thump the man firing the gun on the arm just as the unexpected shot was fired, deflecting what would have been a lethal bullet. The clerk, hit on the side, was spun around by the force of the missile and fell to the ground groaning, a bright flower of blood staining his grey clothes; the other two clerks cowered in the corner, their hands over their heads in abject surrender.

'Idiot,' said the leader, slapping his companion on the back of the head and giving him a firm shove towards the door. 'Get the hell out of here with Per — with your bud,' he looked back at the fallen man, and there was something in the way he paused that showed he was feeling a trace of disquiet about what had happened.

'See he gets help,' he said briskly, and the other clerks nodded numbly, then he pulled away after the men who had already gone out of the building.

* * *

In the meantime, even though it was early in the day, some people were walking along the main street, one or two pausing to have a look at the newly opened bank. The sound of the shot was muffled and barely heard outside the thick walls of the building.

Unaware of this was a woman who was ambling along with a little girl, whose eyes lit up when she saw the partially opened door of the building as she approached on the boardwalk. The girl was about nine years old and was almost the double of her mother, with bright blue eyes and long fair hair that seemed to shimmer in the sunlight. They were both wearing long dresses with loose sleeves, but the little girl was wearing long white socks and flat shoes. She was skipping ahead of her mother, who was smiling a little indulgently, seeming used to this.

'I'll open the door, mom,' said the girl. 'I'll let you in.'

'That will do fine, Lindy,' said her mother. 'Now make sure you don't run into anybody.' She headed for the door, but as the little girl came along, the man in the black coat lounging outside the bank started forward, with a growl emanating from deep in his throat. He had been standing in the shadow of the boardwalk so had not been too obvious to the passers-by. Too late the frightened girl saw that the lower part of his face was concealed by a bandanna. What frightened her even more was when the door of the building burst open and three men came out, in what must be noted was some kind of haste.

The biggest man, who was in the lead, could not stop his forward momentum and fell over the little girl — he tripped down the steps of the bank and rolled in the dust of the street. Lindy had been brought up to be a caring girl, and she ran forward as the man was getting up to see if she could help him, ignoring the sudden, frightened cries of her mother. The man was saying words she had heard her father use when he hit his thumb with a hammer. His head was bowed low, but the bandanna, a red one with white dots, had come loose and was dangling, and the girl could see his face. Still cursing, the bandit hastily tied the loose cloth back into place, picked up his gun, and ran over to where his horse was hitched.

Lindy, who had been bending over to talk to the fallen man, had been bowled over by him as he got to his feet — she fell on her back in the dust and began to shout for help. Her mother, who was also called Lindy, ran forward and picked up the little girl, who had started wailing. The frightened woman ran inside the bank with her daughter to find somewhere to hide. In fact there was no one barring their way because all four of the bandits were at the hitching post where they had so lately left their horses, cursing the world and each other, getting back on their steeds and riding forwards as fast as they could.

This was more difficult than it seemed, because in the few minutes they had been trying to carry out their robbery the street had become much busier. The High Street was far from straight, curving round and up towards the hills beyond.

Where it curved was a Chinese laundry, which was always busy because Greenville was getting more prosperous. Even as the four horses thundered down the road, their hoofs kicking up the alkaline dust, a young Chinese man came out of the double doors of the laundry — he could have been any age from twelve to sixteen, as the Chinese tended to stop attending school early — carrying a bundle of newly cleaned sheets.

The young man gave a frightened cry as the horses bore down on him, a classic case of being in the wrong place at the wrong time. Caught between two of the horses he gave a frightened scream and threw the sheets in the air, the bundle fluttered, scaring the horse being ridden by the lead bandit. The young man fell beneath the iron-clad hoofs, his body rolling over and over in the choking dust — and then he lay still, the once pristine sheets lying on and around him like a dusty shroud.

In the meantime the bandits had

managed to ride onwards, passing the sheriff's office.

As they passed the building they were met by a young man without waistcoat, jacket or hat, his face stricken, who came rushing out of the front of the building wielding his gun. One of the bandits rode close to the man, so close that he was able to pull his rifle out of its sheath on the saddle and use it, not in the classic way because there was no time to hold it properly or aim in such circumstances, but instead he held it by the barrel, swung it like a club, and made contact with the side of the young man's head. The deputy fell to the ground, swept down by the blow that had been given more force by the way the bandit had pulled back the weapon before clubbing him.

'Yehaw!' cried the bandit with unsuppressed glee when he saw what he had done. He sheathed the rifle, grabbed the reins of his horse, dug in his spurs, and rode hard behind the other three as they left town past the sign that said 'Greenville, Pop 3,201'.

The raiders rode into the hills at full tilt: they were empty-handed but their freedom was intact, and for now that was all that mattered.

* * *

Inside the bank the young girl and her mother stood looking in horror at the devastation left by the attack. The bullet fired by the gunman had taken a chunk out of the counter, revealing the lighter wood beneath. Before Lindy could stop her daughter the girl ran forward and saw the clerk lying on the floor. The man was groaning as one of his companions stemmed the flow of blood from the wound with a towel from the washroom. He was a small man and looked up at Lindy.

'Fetch the doctor,' he cried. 'The little girl will be all right here.' Lindy senior nodded in frightened agreement, but even as she did so the girl stared at the wounded man.

'I saw his face,' she said, 'it was a man

like him. I saw him,' at which an extraordinary thing happened: the recumbent man opened his eyes, which had been closed in pain, and stared at the little girl before mumbling something no one could catch — then he closed them again.

'Lindy,' said her mother, 'stay here while I fetch Doctor Neal — just sit in the chair over here!' Just past the entrance were bentwood chairs where the more elderly clients could sit while they waited to see the manager. Lindy wriggled on to one of these, her feet well above the ground, as her mother gave her a hasty kiss and departed to get help.

In the meantime, outside the sheriff's office the young man was being helped to his feet by a couple of passers-by who had rushed forward after the departure of the criminals.

'I'll get them seen to,' he said, 'or my name isn't Brent Calhoun!' Then he sat down on the dusty boardwalk staring dazedly at his feet. It was obvious that he was in no fit condition to give chase.

Further along the street a thin, almost scrawny Chinaman came out of the laundry and with strength that no one could have suspected, picked up the youth who had been trampled and carried him indoors, all the while speaking in soft anger in his own language.

2

Flint was riding home from Afton, a nearby town where he was in touch with Sheriff Couhard, a fat and disagreeable man, but who had given the sheriff of Greenville a chance when one was needed. Flint had helped him sort out some trouble with a kidnapper, who was also a blackmailer, a man by the name of Parker, just a year or so before. The kidnapper was set to inherit all the worldly goods of a prominent elderly local citizen, whom he had forced to alter his will, and whom he had then murdered.

Flint thought he was finished with the problems of Afton, but that was when he was called upon to deal with a gang who thought they could murder local citizens with impunity. Together he and the fat sheriff had cleared up the town. Now Flint was on his way back with the satisfaction of a job well done, and a wallet that bulged with a reward for helping get rid of the miscreants.

The countryside between Afton and Greenville was fairly rocky, with low-lying sage and brushwood, while the trail was marked out by being lighter than the surrounding terrain due to the traffic that passed this way between the towns. It was also used to herd the cattle from the ranches in the area down to the borders during the early summer when most of such work was carried out. Flint and his horse, Beth, were entirely alone, so it was with some surprise that he saw a rider in dark clothes coming towards him; only when she came much closer did he recognize her as his girl, as she lifted her hat from her head and brought her sorrel right up to him before bringing the blowing horse to a halt.

'Katie-Jo,' said Flint tipping his dusty, wide-brimmed hat to the back of his head. 'Well, this is a mighty nice surprise. Guess you missed me more than I would'a thought.'

'You bighead, forget that,' said the schoolteacher briefly. 'You have an urgent situation to deal with. Someone, some gang, tried to raid the new bank. Someone has shot James Dexter, he's in a bad way.'

'Dexter?' Flint had stiffened at the news, his first thought his duty towards the town. 'Why do I know that name?'

'He's one of the new bank clerks, the head one, came highly recommended from Chicago, helped set up the new bank.'

'Sure, I know him, big fellar. Katie-Jo, I'm real surprised it's you coming here to intercept me, 'cos I thought that would have been the task of my deputy. Where's Brent?'

'Brent was hit real hard, he's got some kind of concussion, and he's being looked after by the Sisters.'

'We sure are lucky to have the Sisters of St Xavier in Greenville,' said Flint.

'Yes, Theresa's looking after him right now,' said Katie-Jo with an affectionate smile. They both had reason to thank the brusque elderly sister with the heart of gold who had saved a life that meant a lot to them both just the year before. However, neither Flint nor Katie-Jo had time to dwell on the past — the situation was too serious for that.

'Where did they go?' he asked, meaning the criminals.

'Into the hills, over to the south,' she said.

'When?'

'About half an hour ago.'

They were at a point above the town, because Greenville was set in a valley beside the river, which meant the surrounding area was greener, farmed by locals. The hills beyond rose above the town and were covered in much sparser vegetation. Flint took in the lie of the land with his hand over his eyes to shade them from the glare of the brightening sun.

'Yep, I can see what they've done. We're so close to the border, I guess what they've decided to do is retreat into Mexico, which means they might actually be Mexican.'

'That's another thing, nobody knows,'

said Katie-Jo.

'I guess I have to ride after them.'

'You're going to risk your life going after them? You don't even have a deputy.'

'That's for sure.' Then Flint looked at the woman who had been in his life, and who worried about him, a woman who had thought that things were more peaceful and settled. She should have known better in a place like Greenville, where life was always being disturbed. It was one of the reasons why they hadn't married — yet — and the whole community knew about them and shook their heads about the way she kept putting him off.

'Go back to the town,' said Flint, 'I'll deal with this.' He looked at her with narrowed eyes and set his horse in the direction he would go.

'No! That's not right,' she said. 'You can't just ride after them. They've got guns and they'll shoot you down, you don't even have Brent to help defend you. You're doing something foolish, and

I know you're not that stupid.'

'I guess; we'll go into town then, I'll raise a posse, but I expect them to be long gone by the time they're all raised and in pursuit.'

'That might be,' she said, 'but you'll have a better chance of capturing them if they're still around.'

'I guess,' said Flint, and so he rode beside her. Even sitting down he was far taller in the saddle than his female companion, but as they made their way towards town with only the calling of the birds and the clopping of the hoofs against the dusty trail, he felt she had already outgunned him in some unknown manner.

* * *

Travis Gordon was dining in the front room of the Lazy G ranch, having his usual breakfast of hash browns and eggs fried by Carlita the cook, washed down with several cups of strong black coffee. It was still early in the morning, a time when he would deal with any paperwork that had to be done, and then he would go out and inspect his ranch. He liked riding around on his big black horse, Fletch, dressed like one of his ranch hands in brown work shirt, blue denim jeans and a long dusty brown coat and a battered hat with a wide brim to shade him from the inevitable sun. He was in his early seventies now and he had never been more prosperous — except for the trouble he was now in, a subject that exercised his mind a great deal lately.

There was a knock at the door of the well-lit room. The rest of the ranch had arched doorways, open in the Mexican style, but this was the one area where he valued his privacy and everyone knew he would be alone. At that moment, still finishing his breakfast and contemplating his losses, he did not want to be disturbed.

'Who is it?' he asked gruffly.

'Rosie, Dad,' was the reply. He gave a grunt that meant she could come in, the only person who would be allowed to invade his inner sanctum unless there was some urgent reason. He was not to know that she was there for one simple reason, to see her father, and to deliver bad news.

'Coffee?' he asked, proffering the spare cup he always had brought with his meal in case he had to converse.

The girl who entered the room was in her early twenties and still had that look of freshness that some women keep well into their thirties, with her ash-blonde hair and her quirky, almost elfin features, her curves were in all the right places. She was tall, a solid presence, and silently her father mourned the fact that he was going to lose her one day in the near future to some young, good-looking ranch hand.

'No thanks,' said Rosie in answer to his businesslike offer. 'I'm glad you're already sitting down, Dad, because I need to speak to you.'

'What's happened?'

'I hate to be the one to do these things,' said the girl softly, 'and I know how you feel, how angry you get.' Her father was sitting at a table beside the window — he liked to look out at the ranch that he had started building with his own hands, surveying the expanse with his old but bright glance, and keep an eye on the men — and women — he employed to keep his business running. He was not a martinet, but he certainly kept the operation running smoothly. The girl sat opposite him and took one of his gnarled hands, squeezing it gently.

'Last night they came again,' she said. Her father did not even ask who 'they' were because they had been over such things before. His face hardened and he took an angry gulp of his coffee, an act carried out to avoid saying anything he might regret in front of his youngest child.

'How many?' was all he said at long last.

'Two hundred head of cattle,' she said, 'some of them young 'uns and others pregnant.'

He slowly withdrew his hand from

hers as she tried to comfort him again, and suddenly looked much older than his years.

'They're going to drive us into the ground,' he said, 'if a man can't carry out his business without them thieves doing the dirty on him, he can lose everything.'

'You still have thousands left,' said Rosie, 'but it must have been some operation to get that many, there's got to be five, six of those rustlers.'

'You don't understand,' her father lifted his head. 'Out here we ain't got the lush plains of Montana or the endless tracts of Texas. This is high land, and even though we're lower down than some, the grasses don't grow as well at this latitude. I've heard rumours they — meaning the governors of New Mexico — think we can get as rich as Illinois, but we don't have the variety of plants and the plentiful water.'

She knew what he meant: each cow represented a significant amount of effort for the rancher, far more than one of his counterparts in, say, Oregon would have had to do to produce the same amount of beef.

'What it means,' said Gordon bluntly, 'is that we could be at a point where two hundred lost cattle could be enough to tip us into a place called the red, where I have to lose men, then when the cattle drivin' season comes I lose an amount of profit havin' to pay for shipments of lesser numbers, an' that means we start the new year with a loss.'

He got to his feet, and there was stiffness to his gait that had not been there just a couple of years before.

'It's no use, I'll have to bring in the law, it's a thing men like me don't like to do. I've always looked after my own. Hell, when the wars was on when I was makin' this place, I've fought Apaches with just a Winchester and a bit of luck that allowed me to survive and thrive.'

'You're not thinking of going after them?' asked Rosie fearfully. 'You're the only parent I've got left and I'd rather have you than a few longhorns. We'll survive, Pa, we always have despite some of the things they've been doing to us.'

'No,' said her father, 'I ain't fit to go across to where they probably took 'em, and neither are my men, they're hired hands, not brigands. No, the sheriff and his men it'll have to be.' He looked at her sharply. 'Did any of the men see anything?'

'No . . . at least none of them admitted to the fact.'

'What do you mean?' he looked at her sharply.

'Let's face it,' said Rosie, 'someone, or some people, have the knowledge about our ranch that lets them get the cattle.'

'That may be so,' said the old cowboy, 'but if I start bossing my men around that might cause a lot o' aggravation that I don't need right now. Better to keep them on my side even if there's a traitor amongst them.'

'You don't mean that,' said Rosie, her face reddening with anger, 'let's face them, I'll help you, we'll find who it is, and get them.' Travis Gordon looked at his daughter with an expression that was as stubborn as her own.

'That's as maybe,' he said. 'Let's try the sheriff first instead of putting up the backs of the workers. Let Joe Flint handle this. We ride today.'

3

The Aitcheson and Topeka Santa Fe train puffed into Deming Station and stopped at the fancy platform that few other stations had, where people had to alight at the side of the line. Deming was famous as the site of the Silver Spike, driven in to mark the point when the railway joined the line from the East with the one from the West.

The two men who got off the train were a great contrast to each other as they emerged in front of the main entrance. Neither of them looked as if they would care about a momentous spike, historical or otherwise. The station was brand new and still had the feel of a place that had real possibilities. Deming was the great hope of the south-west area.

'Well Duke,' said the smaller man, 'looks as if we picked the right place to start again.'

'Glad you think that way,' the bigger

man had more of a nervous look about him than his smaller companion. He was dressed in ill-fitting clothes and a dark, dusty coat that would have drowned Judd. His friend was better dressed in a suit with a dog's-tooth check that was not out of place in a town where commerce was the 'in' thing. He had a good woollen coat draped across his arm, and he carried a brown, somewhat scuffed suitcase in the other. In contrast his friend was carrying a large, shapeless backpack that might have contained almost anything.

'Right now,' said Judd, who was wearing a nervous expression, 'we need to find a boarding house where we can settle in with what little we have with us, and then we need to get out and see if we can get something going.'

'We ain't got much money,' warned Duke in his rumbling voice, also looking around a little nervously. They were both in a disguise of sorts because he had shaved off his grizzly-looking beard and moustache, while his companion had just retained his moustache in the Mexican fashion, curving down from his top lip to either side of his mouth. Without his prison whiskers he looked as young as he was, but he was much younger in the head — the reason he had been in trouble in the first place. 'We'll need to go out and get some.'

'Duke,' said his companion, 'we have a kind of agreement here, son, I ain't that much older than you but I've had a lot of experience and I reckon you leave the thinking largely to me, I'll make sure we get everything we need.' He looked significantly at his companion and the pair of them moved across the platform, out of the station and on to the streets of Deming. Duke looked back longingly as they did so at the neat, two-storey building behind them.

'Gee Judd, that ain't just a railway station, it's a hotel as well. Real good place to stay if we have to get out of here fast.'

'Duke, remember what I just said to you? We got to cut our coat according to our cloth, and right now even if we was to share a bedroom the price of them fancy digs would clean us out in a couple of days. Come on.' Judd Nash was not about to hang around and he kept his hat low down, advising Duke to do the same. It wasn't wise for them to take any chances, given where they had come from.

'How do you know we're going to do all right here?' asked Duke.

'Notice something real strange?' asked Judd, answering a question with a question. 'Do you give in? See, all the streets we're passing are named after things they pull out of the ground. Look, we're walking down Silver Avenue, and near the railway station there was Gold Avenue and Diamond Street.'

'So?' Only Duke could impart a rumble that deep to one word.

'Well, that means this area is prosperous, that the folks here have called their streets after the things they dig up and smelt, and where there's minerals, there's money, believe me.' The smaller man strolled on with a slight swagger.

'Besides, I have a good friend in town, one Rodriguez, a prosperous dude I knew back in Arizona long before, well — before what happened to us.'

'Never heard you talk of him,' said Duke striding on so fast that the smaller man had to walk briskly to keep up with him.

'Hold on big man, what's the hurry?'

'The more we're seen I guess the more I worry we'll be caught. I guess I just want to find this cheap lodging you spoke so much about.'

'Looks as if we're just about there,' said Judd as they came level with Opal Avenue, containing plain houses built of the local brown stone. They were more substantial than some of the clapboard dwellings found in the other western towns they had seen from the train.

Now that they were in a quieter area, Judd Nash looked around and saw that the street was a haven, well away from the bustling centre of the main town, and he relaxed a little, though did not drop his guard. He wasn't a big man, and his suitcase had weighed him down so he was tired, but like his large companion (who could have walked tirelessly with a pack on his back for miles) he wanted the situation between them to be clear.

'My good friend Rodriguez, he'll get the work that we need, and if we can keep our heads low we'll thrive well enough until we can get the big job done.'

'What big job?'

'Do you think we're going to live out here in this place for the rest of our lives? I wanna go back to the big city and have enough to live on for all my days.'

'Well, I guess . . .' muttered Duke. Nash looked at him sharply.

'What?'

'Nuthin' I guess.'

'Say it, big man, say it.' Judd's face turned a little red, and he said the things at the back of his head. 'What you lack the means to say is that you think I'm a waster and a gambler, that any money I made would go with the rest?'

'Gee, I didn't say nuthin' like that,' said Duke.

'Well Chance, just like your second name, I'm looking for opportunities, and we'll get a good one, and make that money we need.' Judd fell silent and led his companion to the door of the brownstone boarding house, spurred on by the sign outside that said there were vacancies. There was a pull handle for a bell, and as this clanged he looked up at his big companion. Life was on the up for them, but as he thought of what they had done to get this far, he reflected things could hardly go much worse.

He was wrong.

* * *

Flint found that he was uncommonly busy over the next few hours. There was no question of getting a posse together now and riding into the hills. If there had been any chance of catching the raiders it would have been at the moment when Katie-Jo alerted him in the spot above the town. On the face of it, it seemed unlikely that the criminals would stick around and try again. They would probably have disbanded by now, given that their raid had failed. But then again, the whole event seemed to have been quite well organized, and that could mean that with an aim in mind they might try again.

The first thing he did was to see his deputy, Brent, who was in the sheriff's office but still looking a little sorry for himself, a bandage around his head as he sat at the desk staring at a half-empty mug of coffee. He still looked distinctly dazed, which could explain why he was not the one going around asking for information.

'Look at you, lazing around,' said Flint in a jocular fashion, the smile on his face robbing his words of any sting that they might have had. Normally his deputy, who was young and a little sassy, would have snapped out a sharp reply, but instead he just looked around without a huge amount of interest.

'Hi Joe,' he said, 'you finally made it back.'

‘Sure did, had to tackle a bunch of fellars over in Afton, helping out the local law there, old Ben Couhard, but that’s all settled now, with two dead and another two in gaol waiting to have their necks stretched — and serve ’em right too, for terrorizing innocent folks.’ The deputy remained silent throughout this little homily. ‘So what you got to tell me, son?’

‘Guess I’d better say, Flint, there was four of them, one was built real big and the other three — well, it was hard to tell as they was on horses, but I guess you could say they was smaller and real anxious to get away.’

‘What sort of horses were they on?’

‘Looked like your sturdy workhorses, light brown mustangs, not that big but with stamina.’

‘Were the raiders armed?’

‘The leader, well he was, given that he hit me real hard with the stock of his rifle, but the others, I couldn’t tell, they had on coats and they was all masked, using bandannas to hide their faces, and none of 'em was bare-headed.' The words, when they came from the deputy, were slow and deliberate in contrast to his usual quick delivery, and when he finished he stared at the desk again.

'Did you see what they were up to?'

'There was a bit of a stir in the locals, I had just started work, and one or two alerted me to what was going on at the bank, but by the time I got out that part was all over, then this happened,' he indicated the bandage around his head, meaning his wound, 'then the outlaws took off into the hills beyond the valley.' He gave a groan and laid his head on his hands.

'That's enough for me to go on,' said Flint, 'and it's enough for you to go.'

'What do you mean?'

'Son, the thing you have is called concussion; it means that brain of yours, such as it is, has had a rattling inside that bony skull. It also means you got a chance of damage. It's no shame, you go home, lie down in bed with a yellow novel, read for a while till you drift off, and sleep much as you can — let nature take her course.'

'But there's stuff we got to find out,' said Brent.

'Yep, I agree with you, but you ain't going to be much use to me if you're falling down wherever I take you.' Luckily the young man lived not too far away in a boarding house run by a stout Irishwoman who treated him like one of her own sons, so Flint escorted Brent across to the building, left the young man in her care, and set about investigating on his own.

4

He didn't have far to go, and he was soon out at the bank; two of the clerks were there along with the manager — but there was a hastily scribbled notice on the front of the building that said 'closed until further notice'. This did not create a panic amongst the town investors because they knew that there had been only an attempted robbery, even though at least one person had been shot. They also knew that the deputy had been knocked out cold for a while, and that Flint was just returning to carry out the investigation. This did not stop the sheriff from being accosted by one or two questioning citizens as he entered the building, but he maintained a civil tongue while putting them off in his best manner.

The manager, a gentleman who was in his middle years and who rejoiced in the name of Burton Tibbs, looked askance at Flint as he came amidst them. Flint was careful to take in the blasted wooden counter and the bloodstains that still stained the grey floor.

'This is most distressing,' said Tibbs, 'a terrible event. One of my men has been badly wounded, he might even die.' Flint had a sense that Tibbs was distressed about this more because of what it would do to the running of the bank, than from worry about the actual man concerned.

'Slow down, Mr Tibbs,' he said. 'Can you tell me what actually happened?'

'Well, I didn't see the events for myself, as I thought it would be prudent to stay in my office and guard the safe,' said Tibbs. 'I was also armed and waiting,' he brandished an old-fashioned pistol that looked as if it might have seen military service. 'It's mine from the time I was in the army.' He recounted everything he had heard, all the exchanges between the robbers and the clerks.

Flint did not write anything down.

He had ridden the trail for many years working for various ranchers and he was fond of saying that he kept his 'reckoning books up here' before tapping his forehead. The words would be stored where they were until he needed them again. It was a facility that had helped him a great deal in his job.

He questioned the two clerks, and they agreed with most of the details he had been given, only disagreeing on minor points of the conversation — but that was to be expected when such a violent event had occurred.

Contrary to what many people back East thought, their minds fuelled by yellow dime novels, towns out here were not so violent when it came to the day-to-day running of the businesses. (This was a fact for which he was thankful since it made his job that much easier.) But every town on the borders had the potential for the sudden eruption of such events.

'Do you think you can find those criminals?' asked Tibbs.

'It's looking more unlikely,' said Flint

frankly. ‘On the up side I don’t think they’ll be coming back in a hurry. Now that we know that they exist.’

‘But such a thing could happen?’

‘Probably not, but then again, I can’t rule it out.’

‘I can only say that I’m glad you’re back in town, sheriff, because that young deputy of yours wasn’t a great deal of use. We could all have been killed.’

‘Don’t be too hard on him,’ said Flint, ‘he was caught out the same as everyone else. Well, goodbye Mr Tibbs,’ he nodded to the two clerks and left the building. There was a sense in the back of his head that there was some connection that he had not made between the events of the day. He was going to be busy, he was just glad that the next place he was going to visit was one that was both welcoming and familiar to him.

* * *

Sister Theresa was there to greet him at the door of the seminary, dressed in the usual simple white and black robes of the sisters, her head covered with a wimple and a look on her homely face that showed she was far from amenable to suggestions that her patient should be bothered by intruders.

'Doctor Neal is here, Sheriff Flint,' she said, keeping their relationship formal. She was more than a head smaller than her visitor and twenty years older, but Flint felt like a small boy in the presence of a stern but beloved teacher. 'I'll take you to speak with him.'

'What about the patient?' asked Flint as they walked around the corner to the small hospital that had been opened by the Sisters, years before, when they had created their mission in this very town.

'You know what the rules are,' said Theresa, 'when a person comes to our care we expect to honour that person's dignity and look after them. We do not expect to intrude on their time of pain and suffering.' Flint felt tempted to throw his hands in the air to indicate how she made him feel, but he knew that coming up against Theresa was like trying to push a 500lb boulder uphill — well nigh impossible, and a task that would inevitably lead to grief.

Doctor Neal was waiting outside the door of the cottage hospital. He was a man above middle height who had a stocky but not overweight frame. He was known as 'RJ' to everyone because of his first two initials, and it was rumoured that even his wife addressed him in this manner. He was clad in a velvety black coat, and wore a black hat to keep off the sun. He had a somewhat large jaw that gave him a faintly pugnacious air as he eyed the new arrival. He and Flint were intimately acquainted, since Flint had sent many people his way for treatment — usually individuals whom Flint had damaged with or without bullets.

Neal was smoking a small cigar and holding the leather valise in which he carried all his instruments and medications, such as they were.

'Long time, no see,' said Neal in his usual jocular manner. 'Been a while since you sent anyone my way — what's wrong, you slowing down, old friend?'

'I'm more concerned about my deputy,' said Flint — he wasn't in the mood for banter. 'And I want to have a word with your latest patient.'

'I saw young Brent earlier,' said Neal. 'I bandaged his head; you'll get the bill later.'

'That's no surprise, I'm sorry you live so far from the sea, you'd make a great shark. Now what about your latest patient?'

'I've made him comfortable and I've given him an opiate, it's the only thing I've got that'll help kill the pain. You can see him for five minutes if you want.' Neal ignored the warning look from Theresa.

'Thanks, Doctor. The more information I get, the better for this town.'

'I guess so, but he's mighty sleepy so I'll come in with you.'

'Me too,' said Theresa with a look that brooked no argument. Together the three of them went into the building. It was divided into several rooms, with a long corridor down one side, and some of the rooms had more than one bed. The whole building had the distinct smell of carbolic soap, a faint but persistent odour. The facilities were sparse, but any patient here would get several meals a day, and the Sisters of St Xavier would make sure he or she was well enough to leave.

James Dexter was in a room on his own, the iron-framed bed square in the middle of the space. He was under a linen blanket, and the interior of the room was reassuringly cool after the rising heat of the day outside. The man lying there was big and well formed, looking more like a cowboy used to riding the plains than a lowly bank clerk. His eyes were closed as they entered, and he did not open them.

'James,' said the Doctor, 'I have someone here who wants to speak to you.' The man on the bed opened his eyes and it was clear from his dilated pupils that the opiate was taking some kind of effect as he tried to focus on the new visitor.

'It all went wrong,' he said, with a faint groan, then his eyes focused and he saw the tin star on Flint's braided shirt. He gave another groan and became quiet.

'Hello, Mr Dexter,' said Flint. 'What went wrong, what do you mean?'

'They thought they would get easy money,' said Dexter, 'then they started attacking.' His voice became fainter as he spoke.

'Why did they pick today, of all days?' asked Flint.

'I don't know, the rumours . . . there was supposed to be a gold shipment coming through.'

'Where from?' asked Flint. 'No, wait . . .' he searched the recesses of his memory. 'I remember now, just before I went to Afton to handle some — trouble — there was a message from the marshal of Luna county that the bank was going to get a shipment of gold worth at least $500,000. A lot of money for an area like this one.'

'I guess,' mumbled Dexter. 'Sorry, the drugs; I'm wanting to sleep real bad. I don't have much to tell you sheriff.'

'But why did they shoot you?'

'They were angry, one of them took it out on me when they found out there was no gold, but the rest believed me. They went.' Dexter gave a deep yawn. It seemed that his medication was indeed having a profound effect on him.

'Right, Sheriff Flint,' said Theresa, 'you've seen him, you've asked him a few questions, now it's time to leave him alone. He'll speak to you tomorrow.' By this time Dexter had closed his eyes and seemed to be sleeping.

'I guess you're right,' said Flint.

'I have to go along,' said Neal amiably, 'I have a little girl to see.'

'A little girl? Why?'

'It's strange, to be honest she was there at the robbery, her mom says she was knocked over by one of the robbers and it upset her real bad. I'm just going to have a look at her.' There was a grunt from the bed, but when they looked back Dexter had turned over in his sleep and was breathing deeply through his mouth.

The three left the room and went outside the long building that was attached to the side of the St Xavier Mission.

'I'll come back and question him tomorrow,' said Flint.

'You won't if he's ill or develops a fever,' said Theresa, and she looked straight up at Flint, standing her full five feet four inches high. He knew when to give in graciously.

'You're right, of course; he won't be much use to me in that state anyway.'

'Good afternoon, gentlemen,' said Theresa, giving them a nod to indicate that she was finished with them and moving off briskly — no mean feat for a woman of her width — and she closed the green door behind her with a sharp click.

'It's funny,' said Dr Neal as they walked along towards the girl's house, 'but I could swear the painkiller I gave Dexter wasn't enough to send him off — but there you are, the human body is a strange thing. One man's meat is another man's poison.'

They were soon at the door of a neat little wooden house in the middle of town. It had whitewashed walls and red shutters.

A youngish woman was at the door looking anxiously up and down the street, and a look of relief came over her attractive features as she saw Doctor Neal.

'Doctor, I just want you to have a look at Lindy and see she's OK.'

'I think that can be arranged, Mrs Cassidy,' said Neal with that bluff heartiness that he always displayed. There was something about his stolid frame and firm jaw as well as the shock of dark hair that he displayed when he swept off his hat that seemed to make women melt towards him. Flint felt like a spare part in his own town. He too swept off his hat and gave the woman a faint smile.

'After the doctor has finished ma'am, can I come in and talk to your daughter Lindy? I believe she may have some information that might help me with this case.'

‘Sheriff Flint, isn’t it? Well, your deputy didn’t do a very good job of helping my daughter earlier on today. As far as I am concerned she is a little girl and has had a lot of distress, I don’t want to give her any more, and so you can get on your tracks and walk the other way.’

‘But Mrs Cassidy, this is important, she saw the face of one of the robbers.’

‘Won’t make much difference, will it?’ said the woman as she ushered Doctor Neal inside, and looked at Flint with contempt, shutting the door firmly behind her just to prove her point.

As he walked away faintly shaking his head Flint had the feeling that she was wrong, that tiny things mattered. It was a thought that would come back to haunt him.

5

Travis Gordon had left the supervision of the ranch, the Lazy G, in the capable hands of his head charge hand Willis Jones. The latter did not look happy with what had happened to the ranch over the last few weeks.

'Over three hundred head of cattle,' said Willis. 'The last one was the biggest. Small batches it was at first, we thought it was Injuns or a small gang who wanted 'em for personal use — to corral and eat while they was out doing other things in the district. But this could be bad for you, boss.'

'If I was twenty years younger I would get some of my men together and ride out to get the critters myself,' said Travis Gordon stoutly, 'but the fact is, unlike some, I recognize my age and that we need professional help. Remember, you and the hands are hired to look after the cattle, round 'em up and drive 'em to market. There isn't a professional gunman amongst you. Hell, most of you don't even own a decent gun, just old rifles and one or two service revolvers, enough to keep the coyotes at bay and deter any rustlers you might have to confront direct. You ain't got the weapons for a pitched battle, which is what this might turn into.'

'I guess so,' said Willis in response to this little speech, looking somewhat crestfallen at the thought, but with a faint air of relief that he would not have to take part in any fighting that might ensue.

Now Travis and his daughter were riding towards the valley in which Greenville lay, their way marked out by the very trail along which he would bring his cattle. The time was that this would have been just the start of a long journey for his men and beasts, one that could involve a great deal of privation as they dealt with such things as drought and attacks from the natives and straying animals. That was all over now because of the new Santa Fe railway: his beasts would be loaded and taken to market in an expeditious manner.

'I've heard good things about this Sheriff Flint,' said Gordon as they rode towards Greenville past the green fields tended by the croppers. The fields contained such diet staples as maize, turnips, potatoes and butterbeans. They were part of what had made the area prosperous, and all fuelled by the big, sluggish muddy brown river that meandered past the main town. This, and the ranches like his that had been founded around the area, meant that Greenville was thriving.

A big part of the prosperity of the town was the mining community. Several mines lay at the foot of the nearby mountains producing gold, silver and even copper in an area that was rich in minerals of all kinds. Most of the mines were owned by companies, but the large number of people who lived and worked in the area meant that Greenville was able to support several large saloons and it was a favourite place at the weekend, when Flint and his deputy would have their hands full dealing with mostly drunken fights.

Rosie looked at the town with some pleasure as they rode into the main street. With all the worry at the ranch it was some time since she had been along these streets. Ever the woman, she noted with a faint thrill of glee that a couple of new milliner shops had opened in the main area of commerce showing what were, for this time and place, the latest fashions.

Gordon did not hesitate: he looked for the office of the man who was going to help him out. The trouble was, that building was locked, and even when he dismounted and hitched his horse then went up to the door and knocked hard, there was no response.

'Hell,' he said, 'something funny going on here that the sheriff ain't around nor even a deputy. This ain't right.' He could not know that mere yards away Brent was snoring his head off after succumbing to the charms of his landlady's mattress as his cranium knitted itself together, while Flint was not far away either, having a strange encounter.

* * *

Flint was retreating in some confusion from the home of Mrs Cassidy. He decided that he would come back and see her later when she was less obviously annoyed at what had happened to her daughter. The High Street was busy at that time of day, with horses and carts passing back and forth. He was still on foot because there was no point bringing Beth out of her stable for what was an extended walk around the town.

He was passing the Chinese laundry, which wasn't a place he thought of much, except when he was giving in his pants and shirts to be washed and ironed — as sheriff he had a certain level of responsibility for keeping up a fairly respectable front when it came to grooming. It was one of the reasons why he was clean shaven, for instance, feeling that a bristling beard would make him look like one of the shaggy miners who came through here to buy their hardware.

He had always got on well with the Chinese, especially the owner, and he felt that it was not a coincidence that this was the very person who came out to accost the sheriff.

'Chang Wei,' said Flint by way of greeting, perhaps feeling that he needed at least one person on his side on a day like this.

The laundry owner had an impassive, somewhat inscrutable face like so many of his fellows, but even the merest onlooker would have seen from his downcast air that he was not a happy man.

'What happened?' asked Flint. 'You look as if you won the lottery but lost the ticket.'

'Men that came riding through earlier,' said Mr Wei, 'they ran over my son, he was trampled, hurt by them.' Although the laundryman was holding his emotions in check it was clear that he was angry with the world in general and the outlaws in particular.

'No, that is terrible,' said Flint. He was moved to come closer to his friend. 'Where is he? Is he — badly hurt?'

'Come with me,' Mr Wei led Flint into the building, which had been especially designed as a laundry. The air was usually full of steam and big tubs were heated above sunken fire-pits to soak the clothes. But something had happened and the place was strangely silent as Flint walked through to the back of the large building, where Mr Wang had his quarters along with his wife and his youngest son. The quarters were not opulent, but the walls had been painted in different pastel colours and one or two tapestries, one of which depicted a long, worm-like red dragon floating through an azure blue sky. There was the not unpleasant scent of spiced foods in the air.

'Here he is,' said Flint's host, taking Flint into what was clearly the bedroom. The bed, such as it was, lacked a traditional iron frame and sat on a wooden base just above the ground.

In the bed, covered by a thin, white cotton sheet was the body of a young man with bruises on his face but who had evidently been recently cleaned.

'I am sorry for your loss,' said Flint, well aware that many people did not respect the Chinese and thought of them as just railroad workers and providers of laundry services and as cooks in the saloons and chop houses. Flint had never been that way with them, recognizing that they were valuable members of the community who might not mix well, keeping to their own communities, but after the way they had been treated over the years, who could blame them?

'He is a good boy,' said Mr Wei, 'a man now at fourteen, hardest worker of them all.' To Flint this seemed a little deranged, that the laundry owner was still talking about his son as if he was with them, but the grief was real and recent and the pain of loss could affect someone's mind powerfully.

'I swear I will do my best to get his

killers,' said Flint. 'They cannot get away with this.'

'Oh, he not dead,' said Mr Wei, 'we have many type of herb and agent that work on the body. He still with us, Sheriff Flint.' With startled eyes the lawman looked once more and saw that he had missed the faint rise and fall of the young man's chest in the semi-darkness of a room lit only by a candle on a small bedside table.

'You did this?' asked Flint.

'You see among us there is a power that we believe in,' said Mr Wei, 'and it is the fact that the great healings take place with sleep. He has had leg and two ribs broken and too many bruises to count, but with his wounds bound and the brews we use, he sleeps, he heals. But the men who do this, they do not care. They must be made to care. Sheriff, I offer you my service and will get them with you. Now come with me.' As they made their way out of that darkened room, Wei gave his injured son a small respectful bow, and Flint tipped his hat to the unseeing young man.

The Chinaman led Flint to the back of the laundry. This was where wooden poles had been set up, and these were criss-crossed with lines of thin rope, on many of which fluttered the clothes and sheets belonging to those who lived in Greenville.

'I show you something,' said Wei, 'there is a powerful art we practise.' He went to a corner of the yard in which were stacked wooden sticks about as thick as a baby's arm and very flexible. 'You stand still,' he said. Flint obeyed, although he was tempted to flinch away like a startled pony, because Wei abruptly ran across the yard screaming in a thin but somewhat frightening tone, slashing the stick like a sword.

It took a supreme effort for Flint not to move away from this sudden source of anxiety, but strangely enough he trusted Chang enough to remain still. Chang slashed around in front of and around Flint for what seemed like a long time, but could only have been thirty seconds or so, then he threw down the weapon, raised his hands and threw out a few fast feints with those bony weapons that did not actually make any contact but were close enough for Flint to feel a faint breeze from their movement across his face. Then Chang fell away from Flint and gave a slight bow.

'That is what they will get when I find them,' he said. 'But that time I hit,' he looked squarely at the sheriff. 'When will you send out posse?'

'Soon,' said Flint, a little dazed by the whole event. 'So your son, he will not die?'

'No, for I will save him with the power of the sleep.'

'Maybe Dr Neal could have a look at him?'

'No,' said Chang, 'we look after our own — and that is for revenge too, Sheriff.'

6

Judd was not one of those people who wasted time. It was one of the reasons he was able to escape when the opportunity came, and it had allowed him to gain a companion such as Duke when he needed some muscle to back him up. But it was with a foul expression that he made his way back to the somewhat dingy boarding house in which he and the larger man had set up their home over the last couple of days.

He hadn't been in the best of moods when he went out. He and Duke were sharing a room to save money — not an unusual arrangement in these days when restless travellers moved around a lot looking for opportunities — and Judd had discovered that not only did Duke snore, he mumbled in his sleep too, which woke up his companion several times during the night — so when Judd left he had not been in the best of moods. Now, on his return, he looked as if he was ready to shoot down the first person who looked at him the wrong way.

He barged upstairs and into the room he shared with his companion, who was sprawling across the bed, awake but taking it easy with a bottle of Scotch in his bear paw of a hand.

'Hell, ain't you even up yet, you good-for-nothin' layabout?' asked Judd scornfully.

'Why're you coming in like a rat with its ass on fire?' asked Duke. 'Seems a man deserves a bit o' rest after what we've been through.'

'Give me that Scotch,' Judd sat down on the edge of the already creaking bed and took a slug of the golden nectar. He was not normally a drinker, and if his black eyebrows had been any lower they would have covered his eyes.

'What's the matter, Judd?' asked Duke, sitting more upright and giving his friend some room. Judd said nothing, but stood up and went over to the window. After a while his shoulders slumped and he spoke without looking round.

'I guess what you should never do is decide that something's goin' to be a particular way until you look into that thing. I thought we was going to get some work of a type we could do, and be protected as well.'

'You said Rodriguez would give us that,' said Duke. Judd turned at this and looked at his companion.

'Rodriguez ain't giving us a thing because he's currently buried a few feet under some topsoil on the outskirts of this here town.'

'That's the risk you take,' said Duke.

'We all do,' agreed Judd. 'You and me, we took a risk when we got out of where we were. No, this is different.'

'Why?'

'This here town's the great white hope of the southwest,' said Judd, 'given that the laws been kind of fierce in how they treat outlaws — and we might be next. You know how he died? A lawman got him, that's what, and that same lawman goes by the name of Tucker, and he'll be here quicker than a striking rattlesnake if there's so much as a hint o' trouble.'

'Aww, no!' the big man was now standing looking at Judd with a faint expression of despair.

'See, I had a reason for escaping from Yuma,' said Judd, 'though I've never told you . . .' and he hesitated, not wanting to continue.

'You can tell me, pal,' rumbled Duke, 'I ain't going to tell nobody.'

'See, that's the thing, it's just being able to work around with them,' said Judd.

'Who's 'them'?' asked Duke a little uneasily. 'You got other crimes involved? See, I want to keep my head down, not get involved in all that, it's how they caught me the first time, boss.'

'Well, there's different ways of being caught,' said Judd. 'I got involved; there was a woman in Tucson, a real hum-dinger, beautiful and smart. Arlene was her name. We got married because she got in the family way, and she had a baby, Pearl, a little girl as beautiful as her mother.'

'Gee, I didn't know you were a pappy,' said Duke.

'That little girl, she'll be five or six by now,' said Judd. 'She's growing up with a poor mother and all because I was stupid enough to try stealing from a rich man. I was working, barely supporting the pair of them. I could have done it, looked after them without stealing, I mean,' he put his head in his hands. 'Guess I was so stupid, wanted the easy way out.' There was a dawning light in Duke's eyes.

'So that's why you need the money?'

'I ain't proud of trying to steal again, but we're wanted men. We stick around here long enough and the authorities'll get wind of it. With enough money at my back I can go back, find my wife, my little girl.'

'I can't go with you?'

'Once we get rich we'll part, Duke, then I'll be able to see that kid of mine again, she'll get to know her paw, and we'll be a real family. It's the only thing that kept me going in Yuma. But I was missing my girl growing up and it tore me apart so much I just had to escape. It took me — well, us — years, but we're here.'

'We're going to get rich? But what do we do for money right now?'

'We take jobs,' said Judd. 'There's work moving goods around, there's a brewery on the edge of town, you can shift barrels with that big frame of yours, and I can deliver them. We work, and we keep our ears open.'

'A job?' said Duke. He took a swig of the whisky and wiped his mouth with the back of his hand, his voice resigned: 'So it's come to that.'

'Don't worry,' said Judd, 'I'll keep ma eyes open and ma mouth shut, it won't be for long. I told you, we're going to get rich before there's a parting of the ways. It's just for a little whiles.'

'It'd better be,' rumbled Duke, the thought of a job more horrifying than anything he had heard for a long time.

* * *

Flint came into the main street and looked around. It was time for him to get back to his office. He had hardly arrived back in town before all this trouble started. Now he wanted to rest, get some fried bacon and eggs and a good few mugs of coffee all cooked on his iron stove in his quarters before he did anything else. However, there was an old saying that there was no rest for the wicked — which meant that according to what happened next, he must have been extremely bad.

He was just opening up the building when he was hailed by two voices. One was that of an elderly man, and the other of a young girl. He turned and saw them walking towards him with a sinking feeling in his heart.

Despite his more than mild annoyance at being interrupted in the pursuance of his meal, he could not fail to notice that the two people coming across from 'Ned's', the local diner named after the owner, were a striking couple. The man was tall, old and dressed in black, and looking as if the hot sun had melted all the spare fat off his bones. The girl with him was about a third of his age and wore a long blue cotton skirt, a cream top and a practical riding jacket a much deeper blue than her skirt. Her gloves were blue as well. His eyesight was not poor, and he noticed that she had curves in all the right places. It was the girl who started forward as if the sheriff might take off like a startled jack rabbit.

'Sheriff Flint? I'm Rosie Gordon and this is my father Travis Gordon. We're here to look for your help. We were just about to eat and we saw you outside and just abandoned the place before our meal was served.' Flint shook hands with them both, and he immediately noticed that the girl had a grip with a surprising amount of strength, while the old man winced a little as they shook hands, which betrayed the presence of arthritis in his wrinkled fingers. Flint was not slow on the uptake, especially when there was something in it for him.

'I don't think I need interrupt your meal,' he said with a shrewd glance at them both. 'You two look as if you've travelled a mighty distance to get here, you need all the rest and refreshment you can get. I'll come and talk with you, maybe get a bite too — I could sure do with a little sustenance.'

It was later on in the day and Ned's wasn't as busy as it might have been earlier on. Ned was a small man with oiled-down black hair, who spoke with a faint Spanish accent that showed he might be of Mexican extraction. He gave Flint a brief look, and Flint just nodded without even speaking as the party seated themselves at a table beside the window. The food was fried steak, onions and hash browns, but now that he was here, Flint made the most of what was put in front of him after a short delay while the owner prepared their meal. As if by mutual consent, none of the party spoke about their business while they were eating.

Flint noticed that the girl ate in a hearty, unaffected manner, and he took some kind of pleasure in this — some women were fussy and demanding and picky, but this one just enjoyed her meal. The three of them were having mugs of coffee — Flint noticed that both he and Travis Gordon took theirs black — when the talk began.

'I guessed it was something to do with ranching the minute I saw you,' said Flint when Travis told him they were from the Lazy G. 'I've heard about the Injun attacks in your area, many years before my time. Your name is not unknown in these here parts. It sure takes a lot for a man like you to come and get help.'

'The truth is, Sheriff, I ain't as young as I was. In the day I would've saddled up with half a dozen of my men, gone out and got 'em back,' he had already explained about his missing cattle by then. 'Trouble is,' he continued, 'my men from that time are all dead or retired and I can't put this on to my new boys, they're riders, hands hired to handle cattle. Heck, half of 'em don't know one end of a gun from another.'

'So you came to the professionals?' Flint looked at the girl and at her father. 'I guess I can't refuse, being the only law enforcement in this area, but your ranch is really outside my jurisdiction and I should speak to the district marshal before committing to anything.'

'Please,' the girl, looked at him with big, brown, melting eyes. 'You don't have the telegraph out here, so that could take a week.' Flint remained silent, taking a long drink of his coffee and getting a boiling refill before answering her question.

'You might have to wait anyway,' he said, 'I have a real serious case to deal with right now, and I'll have to be on it by tomorrow at the latest.'

'It would mean a lot to us if you could do this,' said Gordon. 'I can pay you well, too, give you a bonus.'

'That don't matter so much to me,' answered Flint, 'but I'll have to get you to stick around two or three days while

I sort this out. Most of the saloons offer a room above at a good price, and I'll put in a word for you both to see you get value for your hard-earned money.'

'It's no use,' said Gordon, 'we've wasted our time.' Flint caught him with a level gaze.

'I can't promise to go right now, but if I can do it, I'll help you.' At last the old rancher seemed to accept the situation. The bill was settled — Flint put his hand in his pocket to pay his share, but the old man waved him off.

'You're the one who's going to take on danger, the least I can do is buy you a meal.' The three of them left the restaurant together and Flint directed them to the Silver Dollar saloon where they could at least get some decent lodgings for a couple of days. The girl seized his hand before leaving.

'Thank you, Sheriff Flint, you don't know what this means to me.' They were standing like this when Katie-Jo walked around the corner, her hair up in a bun, wearing her plain brown and cream school ma'am clothes.

'Just tell 'em I sent you,' said Flint a trifle gruffly, and watched as the old rancher and his daughter walked away, quietly ignoring Katie-Jo and the look of disquiet on her face.

'Who was that?' she asked as she came to his side.

'Someone looking for my help,' he said.

'And you're going to give it to her,' she said.

'To them,' said Flint, 'to them.'

There was a shout from further down the road and a large man appeared. Flint, who knew most of the men in town, recognized Ben Cassidy, the father of the little girl who had been bowled over by the fleeing gun man. There was a look of horror on his face as he ran to the sheriff.

'Sheriff Flint, come quick, it's Lindy, she's been attacked, and I think she might be dead.'

7

There was a look of grim indignation on the face of Duke as he loaded the barrels from Deming Ales on to the wagon. It was the look of a man who had come to town expecting riches, only to find his hands filled with pennies. He threw the last barrel on to the wagon and stood there with his big bare arms swinging at his side and his huge fists bunched. It was fairly early on in the day, but beads of perspiration were rolling down his forehead. Judd looked round from where he was sitting behind the team of horses.

'Finished?' he asked mildly. Duke felt his gorge rising, and for a moment he looked as if he was going to say something, but the ferment of rage in his mind was like a black tide that blocked his thoughts and prevented him from articulating them in any words — if he expressed his fury now it would be a wordless roar of pure hate.

‘Get up and we’ll do the first few deliveries — we’ll start with the Railway Hotel,’ said Judd, ‘that way we can work our way back here by the middle of the day.’ This was an idea that appealed to Duke. He swung his big frame into the seat of the dray beside Judd, and there was an audible creak as he sat down. They soon reached the railway. They went to a side area where deliveries were taken in, and there they were met by a cheerful railway-man in a black and grey uniform who looked as if he was quite happy to roll the beer barrels down to the cellars.

Judd threw down a couple of large jute bags filled with straw behind the dray. These had to be huge and thick because they had a burden to take. Judd rolled the barrels one at a time towards Duke who caught them in a controlled fall so that they landed on the pads below. The barrels were wooden, held together by steel hoops, and they were too heavy to carry for any distance. As the barrels landed in turn, four in all, they were rolled away and into the open cellar by the railway worker. Unloading was a process Duke and Judd would have to carry out at a number of different locations, but this was the only place where they would hear some news of any interest.

'We got some business today,' said the guard when they had finished their task and the beer was safely locked away, and they were having a drink of cold water.

'What would that be?' asked Judd, who was always looking for opportunities.

'There's a load of gold coming in to be taken to another town,' said the porter. 'It acts as a form of reserve for farmers and store owners, who want to know their money's backed up in the new bank.' Judd feigned a look of indifference.

'So what's it worth?'

'Only half a million or so, but there's going to be double eagles, silver dollars and other coins in the mix, too.'

'So what town is it going to?' asked Judd. The porter's expression became a little wary.

'Gee, I guess I've said a little too much. Should of kept my big mouth shut, we're not supposed to bandy this stuff around.'

'You kidding?' asked Judd, 'me an' the big guy, we've got a load of work on, think something like this bothers us?' The porter glanced towards Duke who was resting on a bench at the side of the station, looking like a good solid working man.

'I guess there's no harm telling you,' he said, 'there's a coach taking it out to Greenville tomorrow, early on, they've got a good distance to cover. Nearly fifty miles over a rocky trail, so they'll get going as quick as possible.'

'Why tomorrow?'

'I heard they're sending over a deputy of some kind to act as an escort for the money — and he'll be heavily armed.'

'Well, that's all good and fine,' said Judd, 'but we'll get back to work — sure wish it was our gold, but it ain't to be.'

He was guiding the dray along Opal Avenue before he turned to look at his companion:

'We'll finish our deliveries fast as we can, but instead of heading back to the brewery we're goin' to our quarters.'

'Why?'

'Duke, did an idea ever penetrate that thick piece of bone you've got atop your shoulders?' Duke thought about this for a short while.

'You mean to get our stuff?'

'That's it; you've got it in one. We'll get our things, buy a coupla rifles from the hardware store, and head out to the desert. We'll get a tent, too. And better make sure we load up with enough water.'

'But we need transport.'

'We got that already, let's just say we're borrowing this thing.'

They finished almost all of their deliveries after fetching their goods, except for leaving one barrel of beer to go with the canteens of water, then without looking back Judd cracked the whip and his team of horses trotted off into the wilds of the Mimbres plain beyond the new town. They were taking the trail, but there were rocky outcrops where they could hide, and Judd made sure before they left that he purchased a couple of old saddles whose owners were either dead or who had traded them in. They wouldn't need the dray after the deed was done, just a couple of capacious saddle-bags each.

* * *

Brent got out of bed and winced a little as a bolt of pain shot through his head. It was the day after he had been assaulted by the big bank raider, and judging by the state of the light outside it was still early on in the day. But it wasn't the light that had made him wake up, or even any particular pressure on his bladder — like many a person in town he kept a chamber pot beneath his bed should the need arise, and the need had arisen a couple of times during his long sojourn in bed. No, it was the noise of a low, urgent rapping on the door that made him awaken to the new dawn. He reached for the gun that lay at the side of his bed, although if someone was going to shoot him down they would hardly ask his permission to enter the room first.

'Come in,' he said, and found his boss standing there in the greyish light, the head of the landing looking black behind him.

'How are you, Brent?' asked Flint, getting straight to the point.

'A bit tender, got a lump under this thatch,' said Brent feeling for the said lump under his straw-coloured hair.

'You fit to roll, son?' Brent turned his neck from side to side and lifted his chin a couple of times.

'Guess so, once I've had some grits and a coupla coffees.'

'Good thing, because you'll be riding out today; I had a visit from that bank manger — I expect you've met him, goes by the name of Tibbs.'

'Sure, I've heard of him. Looks as if he has a few too many square meals a day.'

'Yep, well he's worried, real worried, because, you see, that gold shipment was supposed to be here and it's late.

No one should have known it was on its way, and the coach would've crossed the trail between Deming and here, slipped into town and no one would've been any the wiser. I need a trusted man to keep a good eye on that valuable cargo, and you fit his description.'

'It's a long trip to Deming by horse, I'll need to take supplies and stay there overnight.'

'That's fine; we'll put you up at the Railway Hotel, right where the money's going to be. Just make sure you lay off the sauce the night before, if you get what I mean. I want you to be real alert when you're accompanying the coach back here on the trail.'

'Guess I'll take Silver Cloud then, he's good and mature, but not so old that he'll find fifty miles a real push. Especially if we do twenty-five of 'em, have some rest and recreation, then do the rest.' Brent looked thoughtfully at his senior. 'Will we be goin' together?'

'Yesterday there was an awful act took place,' said Flint. His expression was that of barely baffled fury. 'One of the raiders was seen by a little girl called Lindy Cassidy. Her mother wouldn't let me talk to her. Apparently she was fine, just a little upset, Dr Neal examined her and said that was the case before leaving.'

'What happened?'

'Her mother, Lindy senior, gave the girl a drink of squash and let her stay in her room to play with her dolls. The girl just wanted to be left alone. The house backs on to a jumble of back streets, which is important for the next event. The mother was cooking in the kitchen when she heard her daughter give a loud scream, which was cut off abruptly.'

'My God!'

'She — the mother — ran to her daughter's room. Lindy is an only child, and as she came to the door she shouted words to the effect that she wanted to know if her daughter was all right. She shouted this loudly, and heard a rustle and a loud thump, and realized someone was in the room with her daughter.'

‘Is the little girl — dead?’ Flint ignored his deputy for the moment.

‘Her mother immediately tried to push the door open, but was prevented by something inside — there was no lock. At that moment her husband, Ben Cassidy came home from his work, and immediately shouted that he was going to help his daughter. He ran out of the house and around the back and heard the sound of someone running away through the back streets, but he was more concerned with helping his daughter, because when he looked through the window she was blocking the door, lying there like a rag doll. He jumped inside, moved her, and went for the doctor while her mother looked after her.’ Flint looked grimly at his deputy: ‘The girl was sprawled against the door, she’d been hit with a bottle and was out cold, which was why they hadn’t been able to get the door open.’

‘But is she dead?’

‘She’s alive all right,’ said Flint, ‘but her jaw is hurt and she has head injuries.

Dr Neal has fixed up a special bandage to support her swollen jaw and he's given her an opiate to kill the pain. She won't be talking for a while,' his next words were spoken in a tone of pure fury. 'Someone tried to kill that little girl and would have done so if the sound of her parent's voice hadn't frightened him off.'

'Sounds like he had to take off because her father shouted he was coming round to get in the window.'

'That about sums it up.'

'At least one of us'll be here to protect her and her family . . .' Then he paused at the look he received from Flint. 'All right, what's going on, boss? You got something on your mind?'

'Lindy will be fine, she's getting admitted to the clinic, St Xavier's, they'll take good care of her there. We think that one of the raiders came back to town — an easy enough thing to do with all the people that live around the town. He could slip in and not be noticed.'

'But wait a minute, you know what that means?'

'Yep, and it's exactly as I thought, they're out there hovering around the hills.'

'But for what reason?'

'The very reason why you're going to Deming. You know Brent, it's funny what gold can do to a man, there's something about getting hold of that yellow curse that makes 'em act in a wild and desperate manner.'

'So where do you think they are?'

'I've got my own ideas. We're at border country here, and that's why I think they crossed over. But I ain't got time to stand here and gab, I had to come and see you about the shipment. I've sent a messenger off to Harrisburg — they've got the telegraph system, and they're much closer to us. He'll make sure that Deming is forewarned about your arrival and they know you there anyway, and I'll give you a letter of authority stamped with a wax seal.'

This was true, because the two of them had spent some time there the year before at the invitation of the authorities

to help clean the place up.

'So what're your plans, Sheriff?'

'Guess I'll have to go and find out. We tried tracking down the miscreant who wanted to kill the girl. My guess is he had fast transport, and when his plans failed, ran to the edge of town and rode out as quick as he could, his murderin' mission failed. Come by the office when you're ready and pick up anything you might need. And get going as quick as possible, as long as that sleep has settled your head.'

Flint walked out of the boarding house, tipping his hat to the smiling landlady on the way out. However, he lost his own smile seconds after going out and heading across the road to the locked building that was his own office. Three men stood there, one looming over the other two, and Flint knew that they were not making a social call.

8

Ben Cassidy was not in a good mood.

'When I get 'em they'll regret this,' he said in a voice that seemed to come from the bottom of his boots, and such was his presence that those present knew that he meant every word. Ben might be one of the local traders, but in his youth he had been a rider for a local ranch and he was still a powerful man, even though running to fat a little.

'It is true that this thing must be done,' said Chang Wei. 'Amongst my people there is an old saying, behead the rattlesnake before it strikes — well, rattlesnake he has struck, but he can be beheaded before he does this again.' The third man was much older than the rest, but he stood there with a back as straight as anyone there, and he looked the sheriff square in the eye.

'I have never heard anything as awful as this, Sheriff. I was passin' this way on an early walk when I saw these men waiting for you. They told me what had happened to Chang's son and Ben's daughter, and I don't care for this behaviour around here.'

'Well, are we going to try and get 'em?' asked Ben in cold fury. Flint looked at the three of them and decided that he had to be as honest as possible.

'Folks, there's every likelihood that after all of this, they've disbanded. The attack on Lindy could've been a last ditch attempt to cover up their tracks.'

'I don't care,' said Ben, 'far as I'm concerned this is the time to get after 'em and dole out some rough justice.'

'The problem is a simple one,' said Flint with a degree of caution in his tone. 'It sounds as if they're Mexican, and they could be across the border right now, in Chihuahua, and we all know that there's a treaty in place.'

'What kind of treaty?' asked Chang Wei.

'The fact is, relations between the US and Mexico have always been kind of touchy,' said Flint. 'We go riding over there without a by-your-leave, armed and ready for some kind of fight, and that might be seen as unwanted foreign aggression on the part of some people. In fact it's so serious that if the Mexican authorities take issue with what we're doing, we could all be arrested and I could lose my job — or worse.' He then turned and looked at the old man, and said: 'And you know, Mr Gordon, this isn't even your fight. You don't need to trouble yourself with this, especially with what you have on your mind.'

'That may be so, but I know the Mexican states that border these ones as well as I know my own land — comes of being in the cattle business for so long — and I know the quickest ways to trail. I could save you hours in trying to track these evil men down, and that could be real crucial.'

'Let him in,' said Ben, 'we got to get the scum who did this, and do it real soon. If he can help you get to them sooner, he's got to be there.'

‘Hardware man, he is right,’ said Chang, ‘my son, he could have died, he could still die. We all go together, best chance.’

‘And you don’t need to go, Sheriff,’ said Ben, looking straight at Flint. ‘You ain’t going to lose everything if I can help it.’ This caused Flint to think long and hard — even though he was a man who could take fast, decisive action, he wasn’t one to make snap judgements in everyday life. He knew that invasion of their territory was looked on seriously by the Mexicans, and that a group of armed men crossing into their territory could be enough to spark a reaction from the Mexican authorities that might even reach up to state level. In that case he might end up on trial for crimes against the state, and prison was a real possibility.

Then he thought of the man who had been shot by the criminals, the injured girl and the young man who was currently lying there in a coma from which he might never emerge, and his resolve stiffened.

'The three of you have no experience of dealing with lawbreakers, you don't know what they're like to beard in their own territory, and they seem to have a professional approach, treating this like a job. Even if you're as good a tracker as you say, Travis, you can't respond like a young man, and these two are so furious they might let anger overcome their caution. No, I'm coming with you.'

* * *

Back at the Silver Dollar, Rosie was waiting for her father. She wasn't as early at rising as her parent, and the saloon didn't offer the luxuries of a proper hotel such as breakfast, which meant they would have to go to the nearest chop house. Luckily such places were already open for business because the miners tended to rise at extremely early hours to get to their work, and often ate in such places.

However, she was now clad in a dress that she had purchased the previous day and looked womanly and inviting, catching a few admiring glances from passing miners. Her father approached her with a rather sheepish look on his face — though he had not been roistering with one of the rather attractive women who had flirted with him the previous night in the saloon, although she wouldn't have put it past him for he still had a certain twinkle in his eye when in female company.

'What's going on, Pop?' she asked him, getting straight to the point. 'And are we going for some breakfast?'

'Sure to the second question,' said Travis, 'and as for the first, well it ain't easy to put some things to your little girl.'

'I'm not so little, Pop,' said the girl, 'and you look like you've got something to confess.'

'Well, the fact is, I got to talking to some fathers there, and they're joining Sheriff Flint,' he looked around to make sure no one was listening, but the town was waking up, and with horses trotting past and the rattling of buck wagons, anyone around was unlikely to hear what he had to say. Rosie, however, was quick on the uptake, and she gave her father a powerful glare.

'You elected to go with them, didn't you Father? Well, you have enough to worry about without putting yourself in the way of a few stray bullets fired by a bunch of raiders who don't set much store by human life. You're not going with them.'

'Rosie . . .'

'Enough, let's eat.' In a rather imperious way she took him to the nearest eating establishment and they had a simple repast of eggs, bacon and fried bread, which certainly filled a gap, and Rosie's mood mellowed a little.

'Let the sheriff go and do his thing in a day or so, and then we can get our troubles dealt with, Pop.'

'It was just a pity what they did to those two kids,' said Travis, who related the injuries received by the little girl and Wang Wei. 'Anyone who does that to children deserves to be hunted down, and I know this whole state and beyond from my youth. There's all kinds of justice, and I want to help the natural law.' Rosie lifted her head, and as she looked at her father she had tears in her eyes.

'I've changed my mind; we're doing this to right a terrible injustice. I know you, you're a stubborn old cuss, and you might have taken off anyway with just a written note to tell me what you had done.'

'I never thought that for a minute,' he said, the sheepish expression returning. 'But you said 'we're doing this', and that don't sound right.'

'It does, Pop; you see, I'm going with you.'

* * *

Katie-Jo was standing there with her arms crossed over her shapely bosom. She was with Flint in her home, a pretty cottage not too far from the school in which she spent her days. There was a stony expression on her normally pretty face.

'You can't do this Joseph, you could be going on a suicide mission.' Flint was standing in her front room and gave the wide-brimmed hat in his hand a little sweep of annoyance while managing to keep his voice calm.

'Normally I would say yes, put up a defence, and if they tried the same trick by coming to town again, I'd be ready to shoot 'em down — but I have an instinct that there's more to this than just a simple bank raid. These ones were in on something, and I'm going to figure out what. Now I'm sorry if that ain't on your agenda, but I have to do this.'

'Fine! Go out there and get yourself killed, I don't care any more. You're always doing this.'

'It's my job, Katie-Jo, I just wanted to give you the courtesy of telling you before I leave.' He looked at her, but a statue would have been more yielding. He made a step towards her as if to kiss her lips, as he had done so many times in the past, but she remained rigid.

'Go then,' she said, 'and don't blame

me if you get yourself killed.' Flint gave a wordless noise that expressed annoyance at the way this had played out. He hadn't seen their possible last moment together like this.

'I'll see myself out,' he said, heading for the front door and lifting his hat to put it atop and cover the dark, still vigorous hair on his head, when there was a rush of footsteps and he was pulled around by slim, yet powerful hands. She slapped him on the face.

'You idiot,' she said with a sob in her voice before kissing him as he had never been kissed before.

* * *

Brent rode on Silver Cloud as fast as he could towards Deming. He had washed and shaved, and had had a hasty breakfast cooked by his Irish landlady; then he had checked Silver Cloud, who was kept nearby in the livery, as were all the horses associated with the sheriff's office. The county paid a yearly sum to make sure all the horses were fed and watered, and that a number were available when needed for situations such as this one. He found that his horse was in good condition and that he was ready to go on command.

Before saddling the horse and setting off on his journey — and it was still early in the day — he had gone to see Flint, who had opened his office too. He was supplied with a handgun and a Winchester rifle, which was normally kept locked in a cabinet in the sheriff's office, but Flint had seemed distracted, mumbling a brief farewell and seeing Brent off before going towards the three men and the woman walking purposefully towards him.

* * *

The miles seemed to go fast at first as the horse's hoofs thrummed on the faintly marked trail, but after a while the travelling became a little monotonous, and even though he did not slow to a walk,

Silver Cloud eased the pace as he made his way through the sagebrush; by midday they were ready to stop.

Just before this happened, Brent spotted a strange encampment off to the side of the trail. It consisted of one grey tent beside which was a barrel, whether of water or beer he was unable to tell, while three horses were sheltering nearby under a clump of trees. In the same space was some kind of flat wagon, of a type that he vaguely recognized.

Normally Brent, who was a sociable kind of person, would have made some kind of excuse to call on the inhabitants of the tent who were evidently doing the wise thing at this time of day and having themselves a siesta, but this was not a normal time for the traveller. If he spoke to other people they would ask the inevitable question about what he was doing and he guessed that they would probably be on their way when the sun was less fierce. He was certain they would not be there the following day when he was on his way back with the shipment.

Instead he continued for another two or three miles until the tent and its possible inhabitants were left far behind. He found a shaded spot near a large pile of rocks and broke out the canteen of water, making sure that Silver Cloud had a nosebag of oats mixed with molasses as well as water, and waited until the sun was at a more reasonable level before they made their way towards Deming.

The pair of them finally arrived, hot and dusty from their travels; once he had settled Silver Cloud in the livery there, making sure he was brushed, fed and watered, he made his way to the Railway Hotel where he identified himself to the staff as Flint's deputy. The officials who had brought the gold accepted his proof of identity in the form of the letter with the state seal, and he gratefully made his way to his room and flung himself on the comfortable bed.

It was going to be hard not being able to go out later in the day and sink a few beers, but that was the way of things; he sighed as he lay there with his hat over his face, and sank into a long overdue nap. He would just have to do with a sarsaparilla and hope it was cold and refreshing.

9

'No,' said Flint flatly, 'I won't go with a woman, it can't be done — if we have to protect her, then we've lost the edge we need to defeat the raiders.' He did not address the young woman, even though she was standing right in front of him, beside her father.

'Sheriff Flint, look at me,' said the girl. He levelled his resentful gaze at her, but said nothing. The girl was no longer in her long dress but was wearing long boots, grey jeans and a workday shirt in muted red beneath a dark green jacket. In addition she was wearing a gun belt with a gun at each hip, while her wide-brimmed hat concealed her hair, helped by the fact that she had obviously tucked it up and out of sight. 'What do you see, Sheriff? Some kind of little girl who is hanging on your coat tails? Hell, I've been shooting and roping and riding and driving steers since I was nine years old.'

'She's a bit of a tomboy,' confirmed Travis. 'I guess she got that way being out on the ranch and miles from what you folks call civilization. And she won't need a man to protect her,' he smiled wryly, 'fact is, she might be the real bad one of us when it comes to fighting her corner.'

Flint thought about the situation for a moment: in a corner another armed person might be the very thing that turned the tide for his men. He wasn't a man who was blinded by prejudice, and he had known a lot of tough women in his life, including his mother. However, since it was expected of him, he made a show of reluctance.

'I don't know — one more mouth to feed and we don't know how long this'll take.'

'I can hunt and snare game as easy as anyone,' said the girl, lifting her firm chin.

'Well, I guess it's all right then. Time for us to saddle up and go,' said Flint, which was about as close to a sign of approval as he was going to give.

The initial stages of the trip were easy enough, and they passed through the town. Even though they had discussed so many details, it was still early in the morning and the sun was still a distant yellow ball low in the sky. The air was cold at that time of day and they were all warmly wrapped. This was a situation that would change as time went on.

As befitted his role as the chief tracker and experienced traveller within this area, Travis rode ahead keeping a careful watch on his surroundings. Chang Wei rode beside Ben Cassidy, and it was obvious that neither of them were natural companions. Ben was not a very talkative man — Flint could remember going into his store to buy a new broom for the office and spending at least ten minutes in his company without exchanging a word until the moment of the actual sale.

Chang Wei had a taciturn quality about him that sat well with the quiet dignity that seemed to be his most innate quality. He didn't seem to have a need to talk, not because he was being rude, but due to the fact that he would only speak when he needed to, reserving his energies for the task in hand.

The girl rode beside Flint, just a few feet behind her father. None of them was spurring their horses on, a fact that raised the occasional grumble from Ben, who couldn't see why they couldn't go faster, although he unwillingly accepted the strictures of the trip.

'If your father's willing to do this, I'm real surprised that he didn't try to get the rustlers, too,' said Flint. 'This could be a hard one.'

'You don't know the conditions around Father's ranch,' she said. 'Where the land slopes down towards Greenville, that's fine, but the passes and the mountain tracks on the other side of the Lazy G are hard to navigate when herding cattle. This terrain is much easier, it's fairly open.'

'I'm surprised your father doesn't have more of a family,' said Flint. 'Are you the only one?'

'I am now, after what happened,' the girl looked at her father riding ahead; the old man was concentrating on the task in hand, and far enough away not to hear them talking above the sound of clopping hoofs.

'My mother brought five children into the world — I was the only girl. Two of the boys passed on when they were infants and I never got to know them. I had two older brothers left, Charlie and Gavin. Gavin died in a freak accident when I was twelve. Then Charlie, who is — or was — six years older than me, started acting out when he was about eighteen, wanted to take charge of a lot more, then started taking money he wasn't entitled to. He had a big showdown with Father and left, saying he was going to the big city — that was about five years ago, and we haven't heard of him since.'

'So your brother would have known the whole area around the ranch before he left, including all the difficult trails?'

'I think so, Sheriff — but why do you ask?'

'No reason at all, just thinking aloud.'

She looked at him, and there was a degree of sympathy in the look that he didn't like. He had seen that look before when women admired a man, an admiration that could turn to something else, and he already had a girl who meant more to him than anything. Just the same, even in her cowboy duds, Rosie was easy on the eye.

The terrain through which they were passing had an ever upward slant because Greenville was in a distinctly sheltered valley near the border with Mexico. To their left were mountains known as the Alma-Huec range, while to their left they could see the end of the Little Florida mountain range, which further on ended close to Deming. It was clear as they progressed that they were leaving the fertile lands behind them, as they moved into a higher latitude towards the land of their choice. It was obvious to them all that this was not going to be an easy ride on horseback because the ground beneath was turning stony, with rocks sticking up randomly and no clear trail to take them forward.

Travis Gordon soon showed his worth when they came to a pass that could take them to either side of a rocky bluff after half an hour of hard work.

'They went that way; I can see where they've turned up a mess of soil.' Looking at the direction in which he was pointing, Flint could discern his meaning. He could also see why the raiders had come this way. If they had been chased by a posse of inexperienced riders, in their haste, with a fifty-fifty chance the pursuers could have gone to either side, therefore giving the fleeing men a good chance of getting away. Even if such a posse had split into two, taking both routes, it would mean that the bandits had fewer men to fight.

'Wait now,' said Cassidy, 'before we go, how do we know that he's right? The ground looks just the same to me either side. Ain't it as likely that they went one way as the other?'

'I see signs of disturbance,' said Travis

with an air of patience that he was obviously putting on for the much younger man.

'I say we toss a silver dollar,' said Cassidy, 'fifty-fifty on how it falls, I ain't never met this old codger before, I don't see anything he's talking about, I'd rather trust a coin.'

'Well, Ben, I think Mr Gordon is a reasonable man,' said Flint evenly. He had dealt with delusional people like Ben before, who would threaten to jeopardize a mission. Others would cajole or threaten or dismiss, but the big man could be useful in a fight. 'Let's just go round this bluff and see what's there, and if it doesn't seem right, we'll come back and try your method. How does that sound?' With the rest of the party looking at him, holding a suspenseful silence, Ben bowed to social pressure.

'All right,' he grumbled, 'but it might be a waste of time.' In point of fact the brief rest had been good for everyone, including the horses, so they set off with renewed spirits on the path indicated by Travis — but before they had got round the bend there was a loud noise that reverberated through the air, even though it was in the distance.

The sound of gunshots.

* * *

The night had passed swiftly, and despite being 'off the bottle', as he called it, Brent was in a good mood. He had gone out the night before, and because he was so bored with his sarsaparilla had spent a couple of hours playing poker with some miners. They hadn't seen even the barest hint of civilization for a while, and got roaring drunk on the proceeds of their latest expedition, while he had remained stone-cold sober, winning the pot of two hundred dollars. He had ignored their pleas to come back to the table and give them one more chance, and had retired early, though not before going along to the livery to check that Silver Ghost was being well treated.

No one had ever specifically pointed

out to him a fact that he knew instinctively — that the horse was his only hope of getting safely through his mission. Besides, there was one other thing that he had never confessed, which was that he was fond of the beast, who was as stoic as the deputy sheriff and who gave his all without protest. After a short chat with Silver Ghost, who responded with a few cursory grunts but seemed pleased with the visit, Brent returned to the hotel and rested his aching head.

He hadn't been completely truthful to his chief that same morning. He was still not feeling entirely well, and the trip across the desert had contributed to his feeling of just being generally unwell. Even his sleep had been filled with troubled nightmares, where some unspecified monster was chasing him across the wide open spaces of the New Mexican plains.

The next morning he was introduced to Silas J. Speers, who turned out to be the employee of the Bank of America who were seconding the funds to Greenville

Bank and Loan. Speers was a smallish individual who looked as if he might be more at home on the polished corridors of a New York monetary exchange building than out here in the plains of New Mexico. He wore neat, dark clothes and a tie, and he had a nervous, twitchy manner.

'I am armed,' he said, 'and quite prepared to use my weapon.' This turned out to be a revolver that fitted his small hand and would be about as much use in a real fight as a peashooter against cannon. His very presence made Brent feel like a country cousin, all big and awkward and with little to say. The confusion in his head seemed to have grown in the night, too, and this made him even more inarticulate.

He was introduced to the coach driver, a big man called Philo who was about as articulate as Brent was. Together the men loaded the strongbox containing the gold and coins into the coach, which was pulled by a team of four horses. Philo also had a shotgun in a leather sheath beside his seat, so it was ready for use at the slightest excuse.

'Guess I'll act as a scout,' said Brent, trying to make his voice sound eager. He was feeling ill, and his heart wasn't in it, but he had a job to do and it was going to be done.

The strongbox was heavy and they had been helped in loading it by a young porter, who looked at Brent as they were doing so.

'Guess I'd better tell you, I told a couple of guys who were delivering beer about the shipment.'

'Hell, why would you do that?' asked Brent.

'We was having a drink and I guess it kind of slipped out,' said the porter. 'I thought what's the harm, and it's a lot of money going out of here. Well, the thing is, later last night when I was out for a drink in town I heard that Deming Brewery has had one of their carts — and some of their beer — stolen by their own men.'

'Was it the same ones you spoke with?'

'That's the thing, I don't know.'

'Thanks for at least letting me know.' Speers reappeared at this point — he had been having a refreshment before setting off on their long trip — and the porter slunk off, having finished his job of loading the strongbox with Brent and Philo. The big coachman made no comment about what he had heard, and took his position behind the horses, just checking that his shotgun was in place beside him.

'Let's go!' said Speers briskly. 'The sooner we get this nightmare over with, the better.' He got inside the coach, while Brent jumped on Silver Ghost and patted his neck.

'This is it,' said Brent. 'Do your best, old boy.' His horse gave an impatient whinny and trotted off, while Brent did his best to ignore the wave of dizziness that swept over him; after a moment his head cleared — for the time being.

10

Travis Gordon cocked his head to one side and held up a thin, wrinkled hand to stop those in the party who were more hot-headed from rushing forwards and out to the open terrain beyond the mountain pass.

'There's only one reason for shootin' and that's to hit someone or something. My guess is, if it's them they're using this hour to go hunting. What we do right now is wait.'

'Hell, that's no good,' burst out Cassidy, 'if we can hear 'em and they ain't too far away, then we should go for them bastards and lay waste on 'em.' He lifted his reins and moved his legs, ready to dig in his spurs and propel his horse forwards. Flint saw this and had his own mare trot forwards and turned her to one side to block the way. He made a slight but visible move with his hand towards the gun at his side.

'Cassidy, you idjit, if you ride out into the plains, do you think that warning them we're here is going to help? Hell, they'll just start a shooting war, and I hate gunfights.'

'Flint and old man right,' said Chang Wei, coming forwards on his own steed. 'We ride after hunter now, they learn about us quickly, he alerts his men and they fight, maybe win.'

Cassidy grumbled at this but subsided, and they waited where they were, with the heat of the day increasing all the time — but after a while they could hear no more shots.

'Guess I was right,' said Travis with an annoying air of satisfaction. 'One of them was out hunting for game, deer possibly, meat for them to roast on a campfire. Looks like they've bedded in somewhere, and they have their needs.'

They rode on at a sedate pace as required by the pace of Flint and Travis. Now that they were out of the rocky pass a plain was revealed in front of them, but this was not one of the grassy plains to be found back home, or even the level sagebrush of the Sonoran desert. They were in the upper part of a huge canyon where the land had eroded at different rates. This was a place where red rocks abounded at different levels, while the land in between was covered in more of the low brush that was common in New Mexico. The truth was that they were seeing a more nightmarish version of the land that they already knew, because geography knows no boundaries. There was no clear forward perspective because the hills rose above them on the way forward, then dipped down again. Here and there were jacaranda trees that looked as old and withered as Travis, but with a crown of green that showed they were very much in the land of the living.

'It's a bit rough for the horses,' said Rosie. 'I know they can ride through the wide bits, but we don't know how steep the dips are.'

'I do,' said Flint. 'This ain't the first time I've been here, and they ain't the first criminals to think fleeing into

Mexico is going to make 'em safe.'

'What do you think we should do then, mister leader?' asked Ben sullenly.

'We keep riding, find a place for the horses, then we walk,' said Flint. 'I'm predicting that they'll have found a sheltered area near the low cliffs, and have set up their camp. If they're coming back to Greenville they'll want to get in and get away quickly.'

'Walk? Are you mad?' asked Cassidy.

'You'll find out,' said Flint easily.

By this time it was getting towards midday and there was a significant amount of heat in the air. There was a long dip to the left of where they had arrived, and Flint led them down this to an area beside the low hills, while other pinnacles of stone rose steadily to their left. They were in shadow now as they walked downwards, having dismounted from their horses, and found that they were in a dead end much lower than the surrounding country, which widened out into a kind of open cave with the rocks surrounding them visible above, not allowing a huge amount of sunlight to filter through.

They had seen little of animal life, but as they arrived two deer scuttled past them, and it was obvious that this had been their place of shelter.

'There's goat, wild boar, deer and plenty of flying game around here such as quail,' said Flint. There was some lush green grass growing in the bottom of the minor canyon where they had arrived, and the reason for this became clear when a trickling steam could be seen springing from the rocks. 'The water table, it all sinks down to this level in the rainy season, then comes back up,' said Flint. 'There's places like this all over if you know where to find 'em.'

'Well, you got your wish,' said Cassidy. 'What do we do now?'

'Wise man know that when time is right he take action,' said Chang Wei. 'For now we do other wise thing — we wait.'

The horses were unsaddled because it wasn't comfortable for them to stand around ready to go, and the animals gratefully fed on the grass and drank the water from the spring.

Travis staggered a little and began to fall. His lips, even in the subdued light, seemed rather blue. He was caught by Flint and Rosie before he could fall.

'I'll be all right,' he said. 'The doc, he gave me some glycerine to sniff. It calms down the ticker.' He gasped a few times, and his daughter took out a bottle from his inside pocket, uncorked it and passed it under his nose a few times. Chang laid out a bedroll, and they made the old man comfortable.

'You should never have come here,' chided his daughter.

'Too late, girl,' said her father, still gasping a little.

'That does it,' said Flint, 'we have to get this over as soon as possible. Maybe, in a sense, Ben's right after all. Chang, come with me — we're going to do a bit of scouting. We have to get this over with.'

* * *

Brent rode through the plains that separated Deming from Greenville. A range of hills rose raggedly to their right as they rode, and he was well aware that the sun was starting to rise far above them, while the heat multiplied many times as the day went on. They had met nobody, because it was not the season for steers to be taken to the railroad — the only animals they met on the way were coyotes, wild pigs, prairie dogs and jackrabbits, while buzzards circled lazily in the blue skies overhead.

At last, by his estimate, they were about halfway to Greenville, so he rode in front of the coach and signalled to the driver.

'Head for the foot of them hills, we'll find water and shade there.' The driver didn't argue with this order — riding up high, even covered with a poncho and wearing a hat with a large floppy brim, he was starting to feel the heat of the day. As they steered towards the hill Speers stuck his head out of the coach window — there was no actual glass, just an isinglass shutter that could be rolled down — and looked at the rider beside him.

'Hey, what's going on here, young man?'

'It's too hot, they have a siesta out here for a reason,' said Brent.

'But we have many miles to cover.'

'Yep, and this ain't one of your fancy steamships moving down a stretch of water, this is hard, hot going, and the horses is all lathered in sweat. They won't make it at this pace, and if they don't make it, Mr Speers, neither do you.' The banker subsided and went back into the relatively cool interior of the coach while they headed for the hills. Fortunately they found what they were looking for almost immediately, thanks to the fact that Brent had been this way before — namely a valley that was deep enough in the shadow of the hills to protect them from the mid-day heat, while there was a shallow creek that flowed between the hills, an outflowing from the Mimbres River.

They unhitched the horses from the coach, and all three of the men stretched their legs gratefully with Speers holding his gun in his hand, suspiciously watching his companions.

'I'm sorry,' he said, 'but for all I know this could be some kind of ruse in order to take the money.'

'It ain't,' said Brent shortly, while Philo the coach driver just gave a scornful grunt. He and Brent had already sworn an unspoken alliance. They were going to get this gold delivered and get this annoying little man off their hands as soon as possible — at least that was the thought in Brent's head.

It was a good thought, except he was feeling dizzy and out of sorts, still affected by the heat from the day before and the blow to his head the day before that. He sat down on the step of the coach and waited for the dizziness to pass — which was precisely the time when two figures stepped forward from the fold in the hills in which they had been concealed.

'Hands up, we got you covered,' said Judd. 'Now, if you boys just behave yourselves this can go real peaceful, or you can get yourselves hurt — whichever way it goes is up to you.' His words were backed up by the pistol he held in each hand. Beside him stood Duke, a big man, even bigger than the coach driver; Duke was holding a Winchester rifle and pointing it in a way that argued he had used it plenty of times before.

Now was the time, if any, for Brent to take action. The two had emerged from the hills at an angle, which meant they were on the far side of the coach from where he was sitting. He shook his head to clear it, pulled out his own guns, and ran to the back of the coach.

There was a factor that Brent had not needed to point out when he was seconded for this trip by Flint. Brent was an excellent shot, even better than the man who had been his teacher, and Flint was an excellent aim.

Once Brent was sheltered from the aim of the two criminals he would be able to take them down with some well-aimed shots without having to expose his own body, even if he just shot them in the legs.

There was only one problem with carrying out this act: even as he ran to the back of the coach his head seemed to explode into a million shards of pain. Brent gave a shout of agony, then fell to the ground, unconscious.

Duke, who had heard the cry of the deputy, indicated that Judd keep his pistols trained on the driver and Speers while he went to investigate. He found Brent lying where he had collapsed, barely breathing, and kicked the guns away from where they had fallen from his nerveless fingers.

'Looks like a young deputy,' said Duke, 'an' he looks like he's got heat-stroke. Near to dead by the looks of it.'

'Leave him then,' said Judd. 'We got a job to do!'

* * *

Chang Wei was a small man wearing light grey robes; his footwear was not a pair of stout leather boots like those worn by the others, but flexible soft-skinned moccasins rather like those worn by the Indians, and when he moved he was eerily silent. Flint was no mean player either when it came to action, and the pair of them were experienced enough to go at a slow, regular pace, whilst keeping in the shadows and clinging to the bigger red rocks now and then, for balance and security.

This slow and steady progress was the reason Flint had not brought Ben, even though the big man would be useful in a fight. Despite the shadow they were fatigued by the heat of the midday sun. Fortunately the distance they covered was not as great as it might have been because as they came to a dip in the hills, but still making progress beside the mountain, Wei held up an imperious hand.

'Mista Flint,' he said in a low, sibilant voice, 'look over left, see what I see?' Flint obeyed. The raiders had done precisely what he had thought they would do: over to the left the cliffs had twisted into a misshapen curve making a frowning overhang above a grassy part of the terrain. This had made a sheltered area deep enough to establish a camp, which was precisely what the raiders had done.

They had built a veritable 'home from home'. There was a fenced-in area, a type of minor corral in which the horses were kept. Grass grew around that area too, and there was a bundle of supplies, so it looked as if the animals were well fed. The fence was made of brushwood. The actual camp area contained several tents made of grey canvas. The tents bounded a clearing, in the middle of which was a campfire, on which they were burning more brushwood gathered from the hills. Atop this fire there was a spit on which a pig was being roasted. Flint, who had not eaten a proper cooked meal for a little while, felt his mouth watering, particularly when the wind carried the scent of this cooking their way.

On a fallen hollow log sat two of the criminals, while the other was using a large rock that had been rolled into place. Only three of them were seated in that area, because there was another feature of the encampment that Flint observed immediately.

There was a platform at the edge of the camp that must have taken quite an effort to build. The top of the platform was made of hide stretched across and fastened in place with ropes to make a firm seating. The platform was a least twelve feet tall, which meant that any man standing on this would have a clear view of the surrounding terrain — and this just happened to be the case because there was a sentry up there at that very moment. It was obvious that he was on guard, and he bore a repeat action rifle, meaning that he was ready to fire on intruders at the slightest notice.

Luckily at this precise moment the sentry had his back to them and was looking in the opposite direction, for they were well within range of his rifle. Flint touched Chang on the arm, and this was enough to make his companion retreat into the shadows. They both pulled back from the hill. Together they moved away from the encampment as quickly as possible, and without making a hasty retreat, made their way back to the minor canyon within which their companions were waiting. Travis was asleep in his bedroll.

'This has been quite a strain on him,' said Rosie. 'If I had known how much, I would never have let him come here.'

'Never mind that for the moment,' said Ben. 'What the hell happened with you two?'

'It's not going to be as easy as we thought,' acknowledged Flint, 'but then it never is.' He took a loose twig and drew a brief diagram on the muddy ground beside the stream.

'They have a pretty good view all around and they have a sentry on guard, so looks as though they're prepared for trouble. No use us taking the horses and charging in — I say we wait until it's getting towards dusk, and that we use a measure of stealth, slide through the undergrowth and take our time doing so. Once we get close enough I'll take out the sentry — there's an old saying about never firing until you can see the whites of their eyes, and that's good enough for me.' He looked at Chang, Ben and the girl: 'Chang has this stealth thing in his bones, and he'll come with me. Ben, you and Rosie will follow close behind, ready to back us up.' His face was grim: 'Above all, don't take it for granted we'll win. These look like men who've ridden the range before; they were probably *vaqueros* for some big Mexican concern. They have experience of living in the open, and they're on the lookout for attackers.'

'What if they decide to go back to the town in the meantime?' grated Ben. 'They might think their precious gold has come in by now.'

'I don't think they're that stupid,' said Flint. 'They'll wait until they think the town has settled down. Besides which, all we do is post a guard of our own, and if they start riding out, we attack.'

'So who's going to be the first on guard?' asked Ben.

'You called the shots there,' said Flint, 'so you can do it while the rest of us complete our siesta — we deserve it.'

Grumbling under his breath the big man did as he was asked, arming himself with a rifle and marching to the head of the enclave, taking some water in a canteen and resting on a roomy rock, a look of murder on his face as he thought of the men nearby who had caused so much injury to his little girl.

11

Speers performed the desperate act of a desperate man. He had watched in quiet despair as the horses were hitched up to the coach again. Now he jumped forwards, raised his pistol and fired. Given that it had been nestling in his hand it was hardly any surprise that it had been missed by the hijackers. He aimed at Judd, who was standing a few yards away supervising Duke as he dealt with the horses. The shot went wide, which was natural enough, and it frightened the horses, which reared and whickered in distress. Duke pulled away from them, while Judd was flung on to his back.

However, Judd was a criminal, unlike Speers, and he had been in enough of these kinds of situation before to react promptly: he fired a shot that caught the banker in his left leg, and the banker fell down with a scream of pain.

'Idjit,' said Judd, scrambling to his

feet and giving a grunt of annoyance. He ignored the yowling man, '. . . and see that deputy? Do me a favour and throw him into the creek, drown the bastard. We'll show 'em what happens when you mess with us. As fer you, boy,' he was addressing Speers now, 'you just earned a bullet in the brain and your coachman after that.' Duke moved away from the horses, and picked up the deputy as if he were lifting a rag doll. But the action had an immediate effect, an effect that was aided by the time that Brent had lain on the ground.

Brent woke up.

He bucked around like a wild animal as he was being lifted. Like many who lived in the frontier, he had trained his body to wake up instantly, and although his head was throbbing he had enough sense to wait until he was at the right level to launch an attack. Just as Duke was going to throw him into the creek he came to life, twisted around and punched the big man squarely on the nose. It is a fact rarely noted that when a man has been punched on the nose it takes the fight out of him immediately. This was the case with Duke, who immediately dropped Brent, howled, and clutched at his assaulted proboscis.

Duke had put his rifle on the ground while he was lifting Brent, and the latter grabbed this, scrabbled to his feet, whirled around and aimed at Judd, who was standing over Speers, taking careful aim at his head.

The big coachman, in the meantime, had his arms tied behind his back and was sitting on the ground nearby; the two escaped convicts had planned to use him to steer the coach until they were near town, then they would have shot him, too.

Brent was on one knee now, and fired instinctively in the way that he had been trained to do through hundreds of hours of practice. He fired three times in a row.

Judd took the bullets one after the other. He was not a particularly big man, and was flung backwards by the force of their contact before he even had a chance to fire back. He was thrown flat on to his back, but it was clear from his own cries of pain and anguish that he wasn't dead, and that the bullets had missed all his vital organs.

Then, before he could turn, there was a bellow of rage behind him, and Brent felt as if the sky had fallen on top of him. Duke had finally recovered enough from his injured nose to descend with all his weight on the person who had shot his friend. The rifle was wrested from the deputy's grasp, and Brent knew what would happen next — and knew he could ask for no mercy from either of them. They would all be dead meat in no time, left here with nothing to keep them company but the flies, coyotes and buzzards, who would dine off them for days to come.

But Speers, who had dropped his gun when he was shot, was lying just a few yards away from where Duke was attacking the young deputy, and he scrabbled forward and picked up his pistol, aimed it at the large and obvious target, and fired.

Duke gave a grunt of pain and surprise as the bullet tore into his shoulder, and fell away from the deputy. Brent used the time that this gave him to writhe away from the big man, pick up the dropped rifle in his hand, and take up a position beside the recumbent Speers. He looked down at his travelling companion, panting with effort as he trained his rifle on the wounded but still dangerous Duke.

'Well, looks as if your popgun did the job after all. Free the coachman, will ya? We got to take some prisoners.'

* * *

At first the day had seemed long and weary. Ben Cassidy had finished his watch after an hour, and then Flint had taken over, then the girl. It was as they had expected: no real surprises except for the presence of the occasional wild animal. Now it was time for them to go into action.

Flint had already explained that he wanted them to go in with an interval of time between them set at several seconds.

'I don't want us to be so far apart that I can't rely on you for help,' he explained. 'But I don't want you so close that if we're captured they'll get you as well.' He explained to them how the terrain widened out once they were past a certain point of the foothills. They all listened intently because their lives could depend on what was going to happen within the next half hour.

Then it was time to go. With Chang at his side Flint made his way to their former reconnaissance point, while the others followed several yards behind. He was carrying a rifle, while Chang had a handgun tucked into his belt. Flint looked back and waved his free hand, visible to them in the gathering dusk, then he slipped into the shadows with Chang.

Dressed in his loose black jacket, grey leggings and soft shoes Chang simply vanished, and even though they were mere feet apart it was hard for Flint to know that he was there, and he gave a grim smile of satisfaction, knowing that he had made the right choice. They were not walking as they came to the grasslands, but rather keeping in the shadows of the hills and moving at a half-crouch that would soon turn to crawling on their stomachs until they were within the sight of their target. Flint could see the platform clearly before him and he could hear the man up there protesting at his plight.

'Hey there, Mister Boss, there ees no one out there. Let me down for the night.' There was a ladder made of wood lashed together with ropes down the side of the minor tower. It would be an easy thing to climb down. Being easy to climb down it was easy to climb up and Chang spotted this immediately. The guard had his back to them, and Chang vanished in the long grass at the bottom of the tower.

'No, you stay there,' said a clear voice from the camp where the other three were still sitting, the fire getting low now. They all had their backs to the tower,

secure in the knowledge they were being guarded.

'*Madre mía*,' muttered the guard, just as Chang emerged from the grass and climbed the tower as silently as a ghost. Chang stood behind the man and did something indefinable with his hands: there was a grunt, and the guard slumped down on the platform, with Chang gently breaking his fall so that he didn't attract the attention of the rest, who weren't looking at the tower. The problem with them was that they had become complacent — never a good idea in this kind of situation.

It was a situation that required the rest to do their work. Flint had already heard Ben and Rosie coming up behind him — mostly he heard Ben, who was about as subtle as the proverbial bull in a china shop. Ben gave a bellow of pure anger and soon caught up with Flint, so the pair of them charged into the clearing, with Rosie close behind — so much for keeping apart.

Flint had a fleeting impression of

three confused faces as the attack began. His mind, which he had trained to work coolly under stress, noted that two of the men were of medium height for Mexicans, which tended to be less than that of the settlers in Greenville, while the third man was tall, of Western extraction and well built to match his height — and he was also the image of the man who had been shot in the bank! They could almost have been twins. In an instant Flint knew why the raiders had not immediately dispersed: evidently the men were in cahoots with one another.

Although the attack was a surprise, it was obvious that the gang kept some weapons close to hand even if they were not ready for what had happened. The tall man made the mistake of picking up a rifle. This would have been a good weapon for the guard on the tower, but aiming a rifle and keeping it steady under the circumstances was not something that could be done easily.

The Mexicans at his side — they were

all pulling back as they snatched up their arms — grabbed weapons that bore blades rather than being firearms. One of them held what looked like an old cavalry sword, a weapon that gleamed faintly in the twilight, while the other had a long, vicious-looking knife.

Ben ignored them both and went straight for the big criminal, opting for a personal attack on the man whom he blamed for harming his daughter. This was a mistake, because the leader of the bandits swung the rifle like a club — just as he had done on his misguided trip to Greenville — and while it didn't catch Ben on the side of the head — because he deflected it with his hands — he was given a crack on one of his shoulders that made him groan in pain and fall back. The Mexican with the sword slashed at him, and this opened a gash in Ben's side.

Flint, who had held back, now had a pistol in each hand. He had quickly seen what was going to happen, and had been cursing Ben for rushing forwards. He was sure that he could have covered all three of them if this hadn't happened. He saw that Ben was being attacked, and swiftly shot at the man with the sword. There was a clang, as by coincidence the bullet clashed with the metal. But the shot was close, and the force of the bullet went through the metal and down into the hand of the man clutching the weapon. He gave a muffled curse in his own language and dropped the sword, his hand shaking in pain.

Rosie came forwards then and ran towards the sword, which had fallen at his feet: she picked it up and hit its former owner on the legs with the flat of the blade, taking his legs out from under him and leaving him flat on the ground, still cursing.

Flint shot at the leader, who had fallen back and was now using his rifle as the manufacturers had intended, raising it to his shoulder. Flint's bullet went wide.

The other Mexican, the one with the knife, ran forwards, but not in a straight path, and aimed straight for Flint. It was hard to hit a moving target, and the bullet that Flint fired went wide of this target too. Then Flint felt the blade entering his left shoulder and knew that he had been bested by a desperate man. But the man was pulled away by Ben, who had managed to get to his feet. The problem with using a knife is that it is hard to pull it away from the original target. Ben felled the man using only one fist, but it was a massive fist.

The real danger now was the man with the rifle, who was back-pedalling rapidly away from the main action. Flint saw this happen as if time had been slowed down, saw the man was turning the rifle on them. Two or three shots would be all it needed, and they would be disabled then they would die, either shot or stabbed, and Greenville would be open to their next raid.

Flint had known it might be this way, which is why he had arranged for them to come here with stealth. The trouble with attacking an enemy is that the enemy will generally fight back, and this was something that Ben, who at the end of the day was a trader, had not really understood. The girl had known better, and so had Chang. Flint raised his remaining good arm and tried to ignore the pain that bolted through his body. If he was lucky his shot would hold true and fell his opponent — if not, the sheriff would soon be as dead as the rocks around him. He fired, but just as he had feared, his shot passed harmlessly over the gunman's shoulder. The next shot would fell the sheriff. Everything Flint had fought for was going to come to nothing.

This was when Chang decided to intervene. Leaving the unconscious guard, he jumped from the tower, landing on the ground and crouching like a cat. The way he had landed was to one side of the tall man holding the rifle, with only a second of time remaining before he shot down the sheriff, Ben and the girl. Chang ran forwards and leapt high in the air, bringing his right leg round in a sweeping motion at the same time, in such a way that he kicked the rifle out of the man's hand. The trigger of the rifle, caught by the gunman's finger, caused the weapon to roar into life — but by that time the barrel was pointing at the sky and the bullet went far into the air to land somewhere in the distance.

With a roar the man turned to face Chang. At that point Flint dared not fire his remaining gun because the two were closing in, and there was a chance that he could hit the wrong man. However, as they stood there Flint had a sudden strange thought that he was looking at a man who was almost the double of James Dexter, the man who had been shot in the bank. He knew that brothers often had a close resemblance to each other, and that the man he was looking at fell into that category.

In the meantime Chang stalked around his enemy like a much smaller creature attacking an elephant, and like that animal, the movements of the man were much more ponderous than his stalker. He punched at his attacker, trying to get beyond him, to the rifle that lay on the open clearing.

This was his ultimate mistake because Chang bent low, got under the man's defences and gave him a flurry of blows to the chest. Then the Chinaman drew back as rapidly as he had attacked, jumped in the air again, whirling around once again, and kicked him on the side of the head. Dexter gave a cry of pain, swayed like a tree in a high breeze, then crashed to the ground.

The prisoners were soon secured and Rosie tended to the wounds of her companions using the supplies she found in the tents — in fact more than she expected because the four raiders were surprisingly well equipped.

With the three Mexicans lined up on the log with their arms tied behind their backs, Flint got Rosie and Ben to jerk Dexter to his feet and threw water in his face to revive him.

'Why did you attack and try to kill a little girl?' asked Flint, 'bearing in mind that her father's here and not in a good mood with you.' Dexter's eyes widened and he stared back at Flint, his voice a little blurry, showing that he had not recovered properly from the attack.

'Little girl? That's not right, we haven't been back to Greenville, and I don't know what you're talking about.' He winced as Ben tightened the ropes at his wrists.

'I'll make him talk,' growled the hardware man, a disgruntled father.

'No, stop,' said Flint, and his own eyes widened at a sudden thought. 'Lead those prisoners back to our own camp, and hurry, the night's not far away. We have to get to sleep, wait out the night and get going back to Greenville first thing in the morning. Let's hope it's not too late.'

'Too late for what?' growled Ben.

'Never mind,' answered Flint, 'come on, we have a lot of work to do.'

12

In the hospital James Dexter lay on his bed. His wound had been getting a great deal better in the last couple of days. When Theresa was changing his dressings she had assured him that it wouldn't be long before he could leave. Leaving was not the uppermost thought in his mind at the moment. His thoughts were on two related subjects.

His mind was dwelling on his brother.

'Dusty' Dexter had always been the black sheep of the family. His real name was John Dexter, and from the moment he was born two years after James, Johnny had been trouble. Their father had been a prosperous banker, but Johnny had fallen in love with stories of the open plains and the settlers, and it wasn't long before he had gone out West inspired by stories of high living and easy money. In reality he had bummed around from town to town playing cards and conning people to make a bare living.

Two years before the present moment he had passed through Greenville and found that it was a thriving community with three industries — ranching, mining and farming — all combining to make it prosperous, yet the only thing Greenville lacked was a proper bank. Given that this was the case, it was easy to see that such a thing would soon come along.

So Dusty had gone to see his brother, who at once concluded that it was for yet another loan that would never be paid back.

But there was a truth that no one in his family knew: that James was just as much a waster as Dusty. Things had not gone well for him in the banking business. He knew that the firm he had worked for — Meikles Trading bank, who dealt mostly in business banking — had kept him on the lowest rung of the business, passing him over for promotion time and time again.

Oh, admittedly there had been the

trouble with a girl — he couldn't even remember her name now, and his wife had left him because of the scandal — but that hadn't been his fault, the girl had practically thrown herself at him, and his wife had been a cold fish. He knew that respectable businesses didn't like their employees to be involved in anything that could bring them into any kind of disrepute, but it was so unfair when the whole thing hadn't really been his fault.

Such was the hypocrisy of Meikles that they had continued to employ him in a junior position because he was a good worker and they needed his services, but it looked as if he would remain a junior for a long time. His fury over the way they were treating him, and his gambling habit, which had developed because he was so depressed over the way the girl had treated him, were the reasons he had embezzled the money.

So when Dusty had turned up with a true banking opportunity he had jumped at the chance, and although he would never have been able to set up such a firm on his own, he had managed to get enough contacts for Greenville Bank and Loan to be established.

Not many men would go to the wilds for such a venture, but he had volunteered immediately. He knew it was only a matter of time before Meikles found out about the ten thousand dollars of diverted funds, although they had not done so before his departure. But he had hatched a way to pay the money back and make a huge profit.

The raid on the bank had been well arranged for the arrival of the gold and silver that would make the prosperous people of the community use the new bank as a building block for their business — it was just the sheer cussedness of fate that delivery of the cash had been delayed because of some mechanical failure on the Santa Fe line.

Silently James Dexter cursed the state of communications in this area. Being shot was bad enough, but during the raid his brother's face had been seen by a girl — a fact he had learned in this very hospital.

By a twist of fate he knew where the family lived because he had dealt with the father, and had even walked with him down their street on one of his days off. It was in that neat, new home that all his hopes were going to die once that cursed sheriff Flint got going. Once the girl told him she had seen a man who looked like Dexter the banker, Flint would bring his attentions to bear on said banker, and Flint was no fool — one look at those glittering black eyes and the strange stillness of the man was enough to tell anyone that.

Despite his wound James had got out of his bed, sneaking out of the cottage hospital. The sisters were often busy elsewhere and he had simply picked a good time to be gone. He had found the house he was looking for and had peeked in the back window, and such was fate that he found the girl as soon as he looked in, sitting there playing with her rag dolls, pretending to feed them dinner and talking to them in a low voice.

Without thinking about what he was doing, he had lifted the shutter and climbed right inside. At first the girl had smiled at him, too young to realize what a strange form of entry this was — but then she had said 'You're him, that bad man!' and had opened her mouth to scream.

That was when he had punched her in the face, but she had still managed to cry out as she was thrown against the door of her room. He had reached out to strangle her, stop her talking for good, but then he had heard the voice of a woman outside the door, followed by another that he recognized — Ben, her father.

He had escaped from the room, but the blood that he had left had been his own, not hers. Once back at the hospital, sneaking inside, he pretended that he had got out of bed to go to the toilet and had fallen, opening up his wound again. He had been bandaged and put into bed with a severe scolding from the nurses, and it was true that he had been feverish for a night and a day afterwards. Wounds could easily turn septic out here, and often did, killing the patient.

He had come back to his senses and hoped that his blow had been enough to kill the girl, because she had certainly hit the door hard enough. Then he had heard Theresa talking to one of the other nurses.

'Poor little thing, she won't speak for a while, but the bruising has started going down a bit and she's managing to drink water, milk and soup from a special feeding cup. It's got a little spout like a baby cup; she's not the first person we've had to feed that way.'

After recovering from his delirium in which he was being chased by nameless figures in black, he had time to think — but instead of reconsidering his life and the damage he had caused, one thought rose to the top of his mind. He had to stop the girl, and on a morning like this when very few people were around, his opportunity would arise and she would die.

* * *

Dawn had hardly broken when Rosie felt a tug on her shoulder. She came out of her bedroll and crouched there with a gun that had been at her side in her hand, and faced the man who had woken her. It was Flint, and she looked at him in some confusion. He signalled to her and she walked with him past the tent where the prisoners were being kept as captives, guarded over by Ben. Flint had already done his shift as a guard, so he had slept for only a few hours.

Flint led her out of the minor canyon to where his horse was already saddled and waiting. The air was chilly at that time of day, and the girl shivered.

Flint was not a man with a loud voice, but when he spoke it was with a low timbre and an air of authority that made other people listen to him with respect.

'Rosie, how's Travis?'

'He's fine, the rest did him good.'

'Excellent, that's what I wanted to hear. Now listen to me: let him guide you back and keep you all out of trouble.' Rosie might have just wakened but she was as sharp as a newly manufactured pin.

'You're leaving? Why?'

'See, that's the problem,' said Flint, 'if I go into some long-winded explanation it won't make sense to you because it don't make much sense to me. That Dexter lying there is the reason I'm going. There ain't one Dexter, but two, and I can get back to Greenville a lot faster on my own.' Rosie had her arms crossed over her ample chest.

'You're abandoning us?'

'Rosie, I wouldn't ask you to do this if I didn't believe in you. Trust me, but don't put the Dexter seed in Ben's head. You understand?' She nodded wordlessly and watched as Flint took the reins of his horse and led it away from the camp so that he didn't make too much noise in the early morning air. As he mounted his steed and rode away, now in the distance, she shivered again, but this time she was not so sure it was from the cold.

* * *

The ride back to Greenville was not a pleasant experience for any of the parties involved. In his seat the big coachman Philo had to bear the remaining heat of the day, while his horses had to strain to carry a coach that not only contained two wounded prisoners, but the deputy, Speers the banker, and a load of bullion. As the day wore on the desert began to lose its heat and a chill began to permeate the air, so by the time dusk was falling and they finally drove into town they were all more than ready to end their day together.

Brent went to drop off the two criminals at the hospital, where Theresa was not happy to receive more wounded men. Judd was clearly not a threat — in fact when he was carried from the coach he looked as if he might soon be under the earth rather than on it, with his pale face and shallow movements.

'I'll get Doctor Neal out to see him,' said Theresa, 'he won't be pleased at being disturbed.'

Brent was eyeing Duke.

''Fraid there'll be more than one visit for the doc: this one's going to jail. Get Neal to see to Judd here, and send him over. He can dress our wounds, too, when he's over there,' he winced and groaned.

'That'll cost you a penny or two,' said Theresa, 'and if you're hurt too you should be staying here.'

Brent shrugged. 'Guess the county will just have to pay.'

Judd was taken inside, and then the big prisoner was taken to the jail and locked into a cell, protesting at being left on his own. Brent threw him some bread and cheese.

'There's a jug of cold water in your cell. Eat and shut up,' said Brent. Doctor Neal came and duly bandaged the wounds of the two men — the deputy and the prisoner.

'If this keeps up I'll be able to retire,' he chuckled.

There was one more duty to carry out before the end of the day. The bank manager, Tibbs, who lived in a large house on a hill at the edge of town — it had been part of the deal that he had made to come to Greenville — was contacted by Brent, who battered on his door until the banker appeared. Tibbs was holding a gun when he appeared, having apparently decided that he was going to be robbed and killed on the spot. The raid a couple of days before had shaken him to the core of his overweight being.

'We got your precious money,' said Brent, 'so now can we get to your bank and load it into your safe so we can put an end to all of this and get some shut-eye? It's been a long day.'

'I'll get my keys,' said Tibbs.

13

Flint was an expert horseman. He had to be, given that his life had been built around using horses for everyday purposes, but the ride back to Greenville tested every skill that he had acquired over the years. The terrain was so uneven that there was a real possibility that his steed could stumble on a loose rock or slide down a rill and end up injured. If she broke any of her legs Flint would have to shoot her, which would mean the loss of an old friend and a problem for the sheriff.

This meant that he could not go as fast as he wanted.

Maybe he was too late already, if the thoughts that were driving through his head were true, but he could not let this stop him. He was not indulging in the luxury of hope because he didn't believe in that particular way of thinking. Flint worked on certainty, and he was certain that in this particular case, if he did nothing then a key witness was going to lose her life.

He rode for hours, Beth seeming to go slowly, but eating up the miles towards the border just the same. He and the animal were helped by the fact that after several hours they were able to cross the patch of Mimbres desert that had taken them towards the broken land. Now they were in the foothills of the mountains that surrounded the area, where it was much cooler and he was able to find the pass they had used to get here.

With firmer footing, despite the fact that she was more tired, Flint's horse was able to move at a swifter pace, although Flint was still cautious because he knew that where there was soil and low-lying vegetation it was easy enough for a horse to put its foot down a gopher or rabbit hole and tumble over, breaking a limb in the process.

It seemed an eternity before Greenville came into sight, yet because of the progress they had made it was barely past midday. Flint dismounted and led his mount down a steep slope — it would never do to fall at this stage — and got back on as they came to the outskirts of the town and the notice that proclaimed its name with pride.

He was unutterably weary — the back of his throat was parched, and his horse wasn't in much better condition; the both of them could do with a long cool drink, only in his case it was a draught of cold beer he needed. They both limped on, and the St Xavier mission came into sight at the end of the road, the arched doorway and the whitewashed walls seeming to shiver in the heat of the day. Flint tethered his horse at the nearby saloon and the animal gratefully dipped her muzzle into a draught of welcome even if lukewarm water.

Flint staggered forwards and went to the side of the building where the hospital was situated. The mission depended entirely on charitable funds, and he had donated to it since the day he had arrived in town as a much younger and more idealistic man. The side door was fast shut for a change, and he battered on it with a dusty leather-clad fist.

'Theresa, let me in, it's urgent.'

The door was opened after a short rush of footsteps inside the building, and Theresa appeared. Usually there was some deadpan banter between them, for they were exceedingly fond of each other, but now she looked at him with the expression of a woman who had seen true evil. She grabbed him by the arm and dragged him inside.

* * *

Dexter was lying in his bed: it was late evening, and in between bouts of sleep, he was thinking of how he was going to make his move when he heard a commotion. The hospital had an open ward and only three private rooms — he knew that much from what he had seen on his previous, hurried journey in and out of the building. The facilities were fairly basic, but they were there, along with the attentions of the Sisters of St Xavier, an order who had taken a vow of caring for those who were sick and needed help.

There was no shame in his soul that he was going to take advantage of their hospitality. Indeed, he was pleased that they had given him this opportunity to take revenge on the child who might mess up his affairs.

Now his move was thwarted as he heard the sleepy sisters dealing with the arrival of a new patient. Even worse, he also heard the arrival of Doctor Neal, who stayed for quite a while and seemed to be doing some kind of minor procedure on the man. He heard screams and moans from the patient, and the firm words of the man who was treating him. The whole event — including the attentions of the doctor — seemed to drag on for hours to the man confined to his room, though probably took barely an hour. He could hear Neal talking as he stood in the common corridor that linked all the rooms together.

'I've removed two bullets from his

body — the third one passed right through and I've given him some laudanum to get him to sleep. Leaving those bullets in the way they did probably saved the man's life, because he bled quite a lot when they came out.'

'I know,' said Theresa, 'I dressed the wounds.'

'It's in the lap of the gods now,' said Neal. 'If there's internal bleeding or he develops septicaemia there's not a thing I can do about it.'

'There is only one God,' said Theresa, 'and the man's fate will be decided that way.'

'Oh well, I guess so,' said Neal, with a return to the humour in his voice, 'and I guess the young deputy's just following in the footsteps of his mentor, Sheriff Flint, creating patients for me. Oh well, the state pays and I obeys. Good day, ma'am.' Then there was the crunch of gravel as the doctor stepped away from the building.

The Sisters moved about for a short while after that, and the wounded man, who had been put in the next room, moaned for quite a while, then settled down to a drug-induced sleep in which snoring was the main feature.

Dexter drifted off and woke in the different twilight of morning, and he knew from his days of embezzlement that a man had to act in a bold manner if he was to achieve anything. He got out of bed and almost groaned as his newly scarred wound gave an almighty twinge. He moved with the caution of a man who knew exactly what he wanted to do, and he had been in robust health before that idiot had messed up by shooting him, so he had a lot of strength left in his big body.

The new patient was next door to him. He stood at the door of his room and listened for what seemed like a long time, though it must only have been a minute or two. All he heard was the troubled breathing of a deeply drugged man. The girl's breathing was too light to be heard at this distance.

He moved out of the doorway and

walked along the passageway that lined one side of the building and connected all the rooms. He was wearing only his socks and a voluminous nightshirt, and the morning air was cold, making him shiver.

Dexter stood in the doorway of the third room. The girl was lying there under the cream and grey blankets of the hospital, barely disturbing the size of the bed; only her head was visible on the striped pillows, and it could be seen that it was bandaged, including her lower face, the bandage running under her jaw. She was the perfect victim from that angle because she would not be able to cry out.

Straight across from the girl was a heavy wooden crucifix the size of a man, which had been hung from a hook embedded in the wall. He gave a slight shiver as he saw this, then shrugged it off, as he was not a religious man.

Prayers would do her no good.

He walked over to the bed, the plan of what he was going to do quite clear in his mind. He would pull out one of her pillows and put it over her face and suffocate her until she died, and then he would replace the pillow and sneak out again. It would be the work of mere seconds. Once it was over he would go back to bed and the Sisters would find her when they went about their morning duties. They would have no reason to think it was anything other than a natural death, they would just think that the trauma of her injuries had caused her to pass on.

He was pulling out the lower pillow, which was less anchored down by her head, when she felt the motion and opened her eyes, which widened as she saw him standing over her. She had clearly recognized him. A little child of seven with pallid skin and wide eyes who had never done anyone harm in her entire life. For a moment he wavered, then he realized that his life hung on what she was going to do when she recovered enough to speak, and he hardened his heart.

She lifted her arms in supplication, hands spread out, but he lowered the pillow and began to press down, ignoring her choked sobs. Seconds, that was all it would take, and he would be free to plan his future crimes.

So busy was he that he did not hear the staggering footsteps behind him. What he did feel were the bony fingers on his shoulders that pulled him back from the bed. He whirled round to confront whoever was preventing him from finishing his grisly deed, and found a man standing there.

Or rather the caricature of a man.

Judd was a ghastly white and looked fragile, as if he might burst apart like a broken egg at any second. When he spoke it was in a rasping voice that seemed to be torn from the very depths of hell.

'Murderin' bastard, m-m-murderin' a little 'un, murderin' bastard!'

The first appearance of this spirit from the beyond had caused a tremor in the heart of Dexter, had made him think he was dealing with some kind of ghost, but now he put out a contemptuous hand and pushed Judd away with the impatient air of a man who has a job he has to get on with. As he turned back he realized he had dropped the pillow, so he bent over to pick it up — then there was a dervish on his back, its legs wrapping around his body as he stood up again, the wound in his side throbbing painfully.

The worst of it was, he could not shout out or he would attract the attention of the Sisters and then his deed would be thwarted for good.

He grunted as he staggered around the room with the weight of the smaller man on his back — but even worse, Judd had wrapped a bony arm around Dexter's neck and was beginning to choke him.

Dexter spluttered and cried out, but in a gurgling manner, then he desperately backed against one of the walls and started banging the man on his back against the wall. It was thin plaster over wood, and a huge dent appeared with the force of Dexter pushing against the body on his back.

The wooden crucifix, made of solid desert oak, was hanging there from a hook and came loose, falling on the head of the bigger man. Dexter felt as if a giant hammer had hit him on the skull and was felled to the ground.

In the meantime the little girl had scrambled out of her bed. When the two men were fighting she ran past them and straight out of the door.

She could not speak, but enough people, including Theresa, were alerted by the noises they heard to rush past her and into room.

Judd was still lying there with his arms wrapped around Dexter's neck, and the eyes of both men were glazed over and staring. Although Theresa immediately sent for the doctor, he only confirmed what was obvious: both men were dead.

* * *

The bodies were laid out for Flint to see when he was shown into the hospital at midday. His deputy, looking a little the worse for wear, was in the building. Flint gave Brent a nod of greeting. The two of them would have a lot to discuss later, but this was neither the time nor the place.

He looked silently at the dead men.

'Where's the girl?'

'She's still here,' said Theresa, 'in another room, with her mother.'

'The mother won't let me talk to the girl,' said Brent. 'We had a bit of a stand-off, and I didn't want to force the issue.'

'I need to see her,' said Flint.

He left after twenty minutes in which he did all of the talking and Lindy nodded 'yes' or 'no' with the slightest shake of her head. He took as little time as he could to speak to her, and did so with the full cooperation of her mother, who was an extremely frightened woman.

'The bad men can't get you now,' said Flint, and showing an unexpected moment of tenderness he took the girl's hand, which looked tiny in his own, and gave it a gentle squeeze. 'You have helped me more than I can say,' and he smiled at her in a pleasant way that he did not feel. He had a brief word with her mother outside.

'Ma'am, what your daughter saw will be enough to hang a man, but I'll make sure that she suffers as little distress as possible.'

'Thanks, Sheriff.'

'Don't thank me, thank fate. Who would have thought that a wanted criminal would have been her saviour? Because it looks as if that's what happened. I got to go, but we'll speak real soon.'

'But what about Ben, where is he, is he all right?

'That's what I'm going to find out.'

Flint left then because he had a lot of work to do. He had to make arrangements for the bodies to be removed and taken to a cool cellar prior to their burial within the next few days. Because of the circumstances of the case, he also had to have them photographed. Luckily Al Dixon, the local photographer, who usually took a record of such things, was available to do so.

He also had to see Theresa, who was clearly upset at what had happened in her mission.

'Before they are photographed I will make sure they are cleaned up and made fit to be seen,' she said, 'I know they were bad men, but they need to be respected in their deaths.'

'Far as I'm concerned you could throw them on the rubbish dump at the edge of town,' said Flint. She looked at him askance, but he wasn't going to lie about the way he felt. However, it was clear that Judd had had enough human feeling to rescue the little girl.

It was already late afternoon by the time he was able to get his steed and leave town. This was not a personal choice, but he could hardly leave the criminals with people who were not only new to apprehending suspects, but who had a sick man amongst them, namely Travis. Brent had offered to go with him, but Flint needed someone to look after the remaining prisoner and make preparations for the ones who were due to arrive.

His morning ride had nearly been too late, and as he went back towards the border with Mexico he reflected on the fact that Judd, for all his criminality, had turned out to be the saviour of the helpless little girl. It was a strange fact that even some of the worst people — people who were ready to assault and kill others in the pursuit of gold — had a streak of pure humanity.

His worry was somewhat assuaged when a couple of hours into his trip he came upon the party. They looked unutterably weary. It had not been easy transporting four criminals across the border, and Flint did not point out that in some ways this might not even be strictly legal, since three of them were Mexican nationals.

'Where the hell were you?' asked Ben, giving vent to his anger. 'We could have done with you back there. Getting these four on their mustangs and leading them along in a string wasn't real easy,' he glared at Dusty Dexter, 'and this one tried to escape a couple of times, tried to make his horse bolt.'

'He sure did,' said Rosie. 'Luckily I've been roping and riding since I was a nipper, and I managed to stop him as soon as he tried. I also let him know that he was lucky I didn't blow his head off his shoulders, and he kind of settled down after that.'

'Why the heck did you leave, anyway?' asked Ben.

'He does not need to explain to us,' said Chang. 'The way was long, sheriff needs to take away the badness of these men, then will be time to talk.'

They rode back to Greenville in comparative silence, and Flint marvelled at the wisdom of the man who had once cleaned his laundry.

14

Travis and Rosie made their way back to the hotel, both in need of a wash and a change of clothes, while Flint still had a lot of work to do, making sure that the prisoners were incarcerated in a way that made sure they were secure. The problem was that he had only three cells, and these were capable of holding only a few men, so the place was beginning to seem more than a little overcrowded.

Ben and Chang were useful in this process because they helped the sheriff and his deputy to get the prisoners settled into their cells, but once they were outside the gaol Chang gave the sheriff a small bow.

'I go now and see to my son — if he has survived he will be on this earth for a long time,' and he walked away to the laundry building, heading for his home at the back.

'Ben, before you leave, I have to tell

you why I went away.'

'Hurry up Sheriff, because I got to see how my little one is doin', only reason I stayed so long was because you needed to get those bad 'uns put away.'

'I have to tell you — one of the bad guys is dead, and he wasn't even in gaol.' He spent the next few minutes explaining what had happened the previous night, and Ben's expression changed to one of suppressed fury.

'If I got my hands on him he would be dead all over again. My little Lindy.' Flint looked at him, knowing that soon the shopkeeper would be gone.

'Ben, let me give you a bit of advice. That little girl has gone through a great deal of pain and suffering, and then she had someone try to suffocate her in her bed. Do me a favour.'

'What, Sheriff?'

'Just this, make light of it.' This time Ben shot him an incredulous look.

'The hell do you mean?'

'It matters what that criminal Dexter did to her, sure it does, and you must tell her that he was a bad man who will never come near her again, but what you must do is make light of the whole event. Hold in your anger and smile and be gentle with her, don't let her see how upset this has made you.'

'I don't get it.'

'You can take this seriously, but still treat Lindy in a way that helps her know that her worries are now over, that you're there for her. If you make a big thing out of this she'll suffer nightmares and fears for the rest of her life. Smile for her, hold her safe in your arms, give her lots of hugs, and do things for your family and reassure your wife. Trust me, your wife will help you in this, she's a clever woman.' There was a light in Ben's eyes that had not been there before, and he put out a large hand that dwarfed the sheriff's own.

'Sheriff, you are the wisest man I know,' and they shook hands.

'Ben, you can also tell people your daughter was saved by the cross — turn it into a family story and laugh about it.' Ben gave a weary smile, and Flint knew he had won him over as the big man shambled rapidly away to be with his wife and daughter.

He was going to go back into the office to talk to Brent when he saw a familiar figure coming along the road. Some time had elapsed since their arrival in town, and Rosie had been fed, and had washed and changed from her cowboy clothes to something more fitting for a young lady; she looked pretty in her blue dress, her long fair hair with strawberry hints free for once.

She looked at the sheriff and set her firm jaw.

'Sheriff, I hope you've not forgotten us.'

'I could never forget you,' he said, then regretted the words as soon as they were out of his mouth. He tried to remedy what he had said by adopting a stern expression.

Rosie continued: 'We've had a few days away, but the cattle remain rustled. I think we'll have a night off — Pa's no spring chicken, and the strain of getting to Mexico and back was worse than he thought it would be,' she looked at Flint seriously, and he could see that her eyes were bright with unshed tears. He knew instantly how much her father meant to her without having to be told that this was the case.

'I guess we could all do with some rest,' he said. 'We'll ride out first thing tomorrow.' She smiled again and walked away, and he tried to suppress some of the thoughts in his completely male mind. He had a girl, and she was perfect for him. If only Katie-Jo would accept one of his marriage proposals, which he made at least once every three months.

* * *

True to his word, Flint turned up at the Silver Dollar at dawn the next day. He had already seen Katie-Jo the previous night, and they had had an interesting conversation, if the word 'interesting' meant total opposition to his departure. They had been in her home, a neat one-storey house that had been provided as part of her job as the local schoolteacher. It wasn't the most luxurious of dwellings, but she had made it her own with drapes in the windows that she had sewn herself, covers on the furniture and little knick knacks everywhere.

'You've just been on a mission into another country where you could've been arrested, caused an international incident, or killed or imprisoned,' she said.

'You're real good at summing things up,' he said, 'I guess it comes with the school ma'am territory.'

'I'm asking you not to go,' she said, 'this ranch is well out of your jurisdiction and you don't need to go. In fact, shouldn't the rancher take his own men and deal with this?'

'Travis Gordon, and his daughter Rosie.'

'Ah yes, Rosie, a fine-looking girl. Touch of red in her hair, you like the strawberry blondes don't you?'

'That's ridiculous, there's only one woman I'm interested in. I like Rosie, she's one hell of a feisty woman, and she did her bit in Mexico, but that's all.' Katie-Jo came over to him and put her arms around his neck.

'You mean that?' she asked, he nodded speechlessly, 'then why don't you prove it to me?' His own mind drew a veil over the events that followed — he had a job to do, and it wouldn't do for him to be distracted. He really did regret the thought of leaving Greenville. He had two cases to follow up, not to mention a couple of dead outlaws who would be buried in his absence. Then the circuit judge would have to convene a court, and he would have to be a witness at the trial of Dexter and his *vaqueros*.

But Flint was a man who lived in the here and now, and the following morning all further thoughts were driven out of his mind by the appearance of the older man and the girl. Travis was dressed in black as usual, while Rosie was in her riding clothes, looking businesslike in a kind of 'I'll kill you if you get in my way' kind of manner. This and her curves made her an object of desire to a man who had been hardened by his job. But once more he was able to put this to the back of his mind and concentrate on the task that lay before them.

'Good morning,' said Rosie.

'Mornin',' said Travis tipping his hat. The two of them went to the livery, finding that their horses had been well fed and rested and were ready for the journey, and led them out to the main street.

As they went out to the street they found not one, but two men waiting for them, the other person being Chang Wei. He gave Rosie a small bow as she appeared, and she favoured him with a bright, genuine smile that made Flint wish he had been the recipient.

'Miss Rosie, I help you with rustling problem.'

'But what about your son?'

'I spent the night and some of today

with Wang, he is with my wife now and she is talking to him. He has woken, he talks, but he still recovers from injury. I owe sheriff a favour. I come with you.'

'Thanks,' said Flint, meaning what he said.

'Your son needs you,' said Rosie.

'This fight mine too, if yours,' said Chang, smiling faintly, but with an air of determination that showed he was not going to be budged.

Soon all four of them were riding out of Greenville in a different direction from the one they had taken over the previous few days. While they were riding through the valley and then making their way to the upper slopes, Travis quietly but firmly questioned the sheriff about what had happened the previous day.

Flint explained that he had worked out what was likely to happen to the young girl, and that because she was in some danger, he had felt compelled to ride and save her — and with that, Travis seemed to relax.

'Some of the party — I won't say who — reckoned that you were making tracks so you could get back and relax while the rest of us did the dirty work, while all the time you were acting in high regard for the citizens of your town.' Flint knew well that the person Travis was talking about was Ben, but he said nothing. The big store manager had certainly changed his tune when he found out the facts.

The journey was long enough, taking them away from the waters of the river and back to them again by a winding route, but this time much higher than before so that the air had a different feel, somehow lighter, while the landscape around them became a great deal more arid. Yet because they were close to water, here and there could be found patches of green meadow. It wasn't long before they came upon some cattle on the lower slopes of the hills, and Travis looked at these with great pride. He had spent his whole life in the cattle business, and these steers were the product of many years of work — he could practically name every single animal.

The Lazy G was a working ranch, so when they arrived they found there was a great deal of activity going on, with men dealing with feed supplies, and equipment coming and going. On the outskirts of the ranch there was a corral and stables, some cattle-holding pens, feed sheds and several barns. The ranch also had a couple of bunkhouses where the men would sleep at night after a long day out in the open.

Standing somewhat in the middle of this mixture of structures was the ranch building. It was two storeys high, Lazy G and had been added to over the years. It was largely made of wood and whitewashed, but had a stone chimney butte running up the middle. It had a long porch raised off the ground so that people had to climb a few steps to get up to the front door. Just outside the building there was a hitching post and a long wooden trough filled with water, from which the horses drank long and gratefully. Travis dismounted somewhat stiffly and led the human members of the expedition up the steps and into his home.

They did not have much time to enjoy the hospitality of the ranch house. Rose, who was the youngest and fittest, went away to the kitchen, and it wasn't long before she rustled up some coffee and some food for them. Luckily someone had thought to restock the larder, and there was plenty to eat.

There was a dining table in the middle of the roomy front of the house, which had been created on an open plan, with the brown-painted stairway in the middle of the building. The Spanish-style arches and the beaded curtains leading to the cooking area showed the influence of their Mexican neighbours, as did the fact that the meat Rosie served was spiced.

The dining table was made of highly polished pine with four matching chairs, and they all ate around this in comparative silence.

‘This used to be the family table,’ said Travis a little meditatively at one point, ‘the four of us gettin’ breakfast before goin’ out to a day’s work.’

Flint said nothing, but his eyes and ears were taking in everything. He had a quality of stillness about him that made him a perfect observer.

There was a knock at the front door; Rosie answered, and a man of medium height appeared, a little dusty from working with the cattle — he held his hat with both hands, shaking it a little.

‘Boss, sure glad to see you back.’

‘Glad to be here, Willis, even under these circumstances.’

‘Took your time comin’ back, some of us were thinking of ridin’ after you.’ He didn’t have to go into any details.

‘More steers gone?’

‘Yep, fifty this time, and that’s bad enough, even though less than before, but it’s worse than that.’

‘What happened?’

‘It’s old Abner, he got in their way, so they shot him.’

'No! Abner's been with me since the early days,' the old rancher looked more agitated than they had seen him before. 'Is he dead?' Luke had the grace to seem a little ashamed of his words.

'Truth is he wasn't shot that bad, it's a flesh wound to the leg and it's been dressed, looks as if he'll be up and about in a fortnight. Still, it's bad enough, some of the men are talking about leaving, and once you lose hands — not me — and the rumours spread, it'll be real bad, real bad for business.'

It seemed that Willis had a talent for stating the obvious. Travis thanked him for appearing and sent him back to his duties. He finished what little was left of his meal, then started to go out of the building, only to find his way barred by Rosie.

'What the heck are you doing, daughter?'

'Where are you going, Pops?'

'To see Abner.'

'Abner can wait, you heard Luke, he's fine, and you can see him when the rest of us are out looking for the rustlers.'

'What did you say?'

'You old coyote, you've been travelling hard the last few days, you aren't well, what you're going to do right now is go for some shuteye.'

'Abner needs to see me, and what's this about seeing him when the rest of you are off looking for those assholes who're stealing my livelihood? I'm going with you, young lady.'

'No you're not, you're not a young man and that heart condition of yours could easily finish you off if this continues. Besides, you heard Luke, they're shooting at our men now, and you could easily be one of their targets.'

'If we had 'taters we could make fries,' said Travis with a look of scorn.

'Pops, go upstairs and rest and see Abner after you sleep, a couple of hours won't make any difference. He's not expecting you or anything,'

'I guess . . .' The old rancher wavered — he did indeed seem tired, and his lips were a faint blue once more. 'See you fellers later,' he said with a nod to Flint and Chang. He stood bolt upright, but his feet slurred against the treads as he climbed the stairs, while his daughter supported him to get to the roomy bedroom he had shared for so many years with his long-dead wife.

Down below the two men said nothing to each other about what they had just seen. They knew a man didn't like having his problems talked about. Rosie joined them just a few minutes later. There was a becoming flush to her face from the effort of getting her father to his rest, and her mood seemed much lighter.

'That's got rid of the stubborn old cuss, now it's time to talk.'

15

Three horses set off the next morning. This was a miracle in itself, because Travis, when he awoke, had been vocal about going, and it had taken the intervention of Flint to make him stay. No one knew what the sheriff had said to the elderly rancher, because they had met in private to have their discussion — all they knew was that when they were finished, Travis had agreed to stay, albeit with some reluctance. He was there as they set off, and he had one final warning for them.

'When you and Mr Wei come close to the rustlers I want you to leave my girl in some sheltered place, she's not to do any fighting.' Rosie was about to open her mouth and protest at this, but Flint gave her a deadpan look that made her close her mouth and look away.

'Yep, Mr Gordon, I'll make sure your girl is well protected, don't you worry about that, sir.'

Travis stood and watched them leave until they were mere dots in the distance, then he went to see his old friend Abner. He was going to promise him a raise after all this was over. Being shot just for doing his job was something that no man should face.

'I know this area like you know Greenville,' said Rosie speaking to both men as the three of them rode along.

'You are wise woman,' said Chang with an air of open admiration that brought a faint flush to her cheeks.

'Do you really?' asked Flint as they proceeded on the open plain before the hills. 'So can you tell us the most likely place for them to hole up?'

'I think they'll go to Skeleton Canyon,' said Rosie with a confident air. 'It's a little ways south-east of here, about a day's ride, far enough off that they could rest up there with our steers, but not so far that they have to ride for days to get to the ranch to carry out their thieving practices.'

'Then lead on and take us there.'

'It's not as simple as that, as you know full well, Sheriff — they're going to have lookouts who will see anyone coming, and who will warn them well in advance.'

'Well, what's the situation?'

'There's a narrow pass that leads to the canyon, just as there is in so many others; it slopes downwards, naturally enough. Because of the water table rising from below there's more vegetation in the area, a few pine trees, but it's still pretty sparse at the entrance to the canyon.'

'Have you been there before?' He sensed a slight hesitation in her before she answered.

'Gee, when I was a young girl and stupid I came out this way with Chuck, and we roved around this area for days at a time. We camped up with friends and shot game and lived the wild life. It taught me a lot about how to survive in the wild, and it made me a better horsewoman.'

'What did your father think of that?'

'He punished me by making me stay in my room for days on end — I thought I hated him then I was about fourteen. But it was worse for Chuck, Dad gave him a good hiding. He comes from the old school, does Pa, he believes in that old saw from the Bible about 'spare the rod and spoil the child'.

'Did it work?' The girl hesitated.

'I don't want to talk about it,' she said, and they rode on in silence for a while. By unspoken, mutual consent they stopped at a point where the rocky surfaces became jumbled, and found a hollow where they were able to pitch their camp behind a spur that concealed the hollow from the faint trail that marked the way to Skeleton Canyon. This meant that they would be riding light when they actually made their way into the region. The very name of the place did not bode well for travellers, and it was interesting to find that on the very place they chose as their camp was a ruined dwelling, a cabin that had been built from the local pine wood.

'It's called Skeleton Canyon because in the very early days there was a rumour that there was gold in the region. What they found was a mess of caves and blind alleys, along with coyotes, mountain lions, wild dogs and disease. A lot of them were killed, while others succumbed to yellow fever and left their bones behind — hence the name.'

This was not encouraging, but it was also an indication of what they had to do. They had to get in without being seen and arrest the rustlers — there could be any number of them. But if, as the girl indicated, there wasn't much in the way of comfort in the canyon, few men would stay there for long periods of time just so they could profit from stealing cattle, even if the numbers were in the hundreds.

They were just contemplating what they would have to do, when there was the sound of horse hoofs nearby the camp. Flint walked out with a Colt 45 in either hand. He was heavily armed because he was not going to take any chances. A man dressed in black with a wide-brimmed hat and the stiffness of age upon him, dismounted from his horse and walked forwards towards them.

'Now ain't you going to offer me a drink?' asked Travis mildly.

Rosie turned the air a few different colours with the language she had learned growing up amidst a bunch of cattle herders, but the upshot of it was that there was nothing she could do. If she insisted in taking her father back to the ranch, there was the little problem that he might refuse to accompany her, and precious time would be lost even if he agreed to go. In addition, if she left, it would leave the sheriff and his companion alone to face however many rustlers were out there, meaning the mission would be dangerously underpowered.

'I ain't here to cause trouble,' said Travis, as he drank some of the coffee that had been brewed over a campfire just before his arrival, 'I'm here for a purpose. I waited until you were gone and simply took Lightning — one of my best hosses — and followed your tracks.'

'Begging your pardon Mr Gordon,' said Flint, 'but you ain't as spry as you used to be, so what makes you think you can manage this mission?'

'Son, I may not be 'spry' as you put it so well, but I still got the ability to think, and I can be there as a guard when you carry out your task. He too serves who only stands and waits, and when I'm on Lightning I'm as mobile as any of you.'

'You old fool,' said Rosie, 'I oughter get Chang and Flint to tie you up and throw you in one of these tents until this whole thing is over.'

'I'd like to see them try,' said Travis mildly, indicating the gun at his side. 'I can still draw real fast, as a few Injuns could testify.'

'This is going round in circles,' said Flint, 'I suggest that you just accept your father is part of this mission, Rosie, and we'll decide what we're going to do right now.'

They had a long discussion about the

ins and outs of what was going to be done. The rules of the area might apply, suggested Flint, in that the rustlers might have their afternoon siesta and eat not long afterwards. That would be a good time for them to enter the canyon and take the enemy unawares.

They had plenty of weapons with them. Flint was armed with a Winchester '73, a good weapon to have in distance fighting, his guns holstered on either side, along with a bullet belt around his hips. Rosie had a gun at either hip, with a knife in her boot, so she was armed in a similar way to the sheriff. Gunmen rarely went without a knife in these parts for the very good reason that a gun could jam and wasn't much use in close-up combat.

Chang was armed, too. He carried with him a sword, not like one of those curved weapons used by the cavalry, but a short weapon called a kitana that was strapped to his hip with a cord and kept in a wooden sheath covered in black and red abstract designs. He also carried a knife, but he had no guns. He was lightly clad in his grey robe, and wore a cloth tied around his head with a black string, rather than a hat, like the others. Travis was armed with his old army guns, the ones he had relied on for years, and he too carried a rifle, a new Remington that was his pride and joy, and which he had yet to use against human enemies.

None of those present were arrogant enough to think that the weapons they bore made them invincible. When the enemy was not quantified it was wise to be cautious.

'Well, it won't be too hot to stir in an hour or so,' said Flint, 'so that's when we make our move.'

16

Jumpin' Jones, real name Jack, was not a happy man. He had been given guard duty near the head of the canyon. At his side was something that he had been trained in using: an old-fashioned brass bugle as used by the cavalry. The truth was, a man shouting or fighting might make a sound that would be lost in the mouth of the canyon before which he was situated, but the horn had a piercing sound that blew a warning for all to hear, clear, loud and strong. Jones was cursing his luck at being left up here, chafing at being the one to be nominated for the guard duty they all hated, but which was so necessary given that a posse could appear at any time — and their leader, CJ as he liked to be known, was not someone who was about to become complacent.

There was a convenient stone platform outside the canyon, behind which grew a couple of straggly pine trees; it could be reached by a man climbing steadily up the rough sides. No one could approach from behind unless they were prepared to slide down a very steep hill, which left only the slopes on the other side of the entrance or the main approach to the canyon.

Jumpin' Jones' only consolation was a bottle of beer that he had managed to purloin from their meagre store. It was indeed a small consolation since it had little in the way of fizz and it was warm, but it was something to go with his meal of green lettuce and slightly charred meat.

He heard a sound to his right and looked over — and saw a man scrabbling over the rocks at an incredible pace, and what was more, the man was hooded against the sun and carrying a knife in his teeth! Jack was armed with a rifle, but he remembered his duty and raised the bugle to his lips to sound the warning that would echo around the canyon. But just as he did so, the berobed creature reached the platform, there was a flurry of motion as the attacker seemed to levitate into the air and whirled around, and then a leather-clad foot kicked the bugle away from his lips and out of his hand. The instrument clattered down the side of the stony platform, hardly making any sound at all. But Chang, for he was the attacker, was not about to rest on his laurels, as the guard had staggered back and managed to pick up his rife — and all the martial art skills in the world would not combat a bullet in the head.

Chang ran forwards as fast as before, and his fists moved rapidly at what seemed like an inhuman speed so they were a blur as they caught the man in the chest and abdomen. Jack gave another cry, this time one of pain rather than fright, then a moan that seemed to come from the soles of his boots, and he collapsed to the ground.

Moments later he was bound and gagged and dragged underneath the straggly pine trees that had once been his shelter from the heat of the day. They continued to perform this purpose.

'Good work, Chang,' said Flint, and the Chinaman gave a slight bow. He was panting a little and there was a slight gleam in his eyes as of one who had fulfilled his purpose. 'Now we should go in.' Flint was speaking barely above a whisper, he did not want the slightest chance of them being heard. The noise of the guard being attacked might have alerted the rustlers anyway, but Chang had been wise to use only his body as a weapon, keeping any noise to a minimum.

Together the four of them walked into Skeleton Canyon.

* * *

There had been a guard in front of the canyon for a very good reason. It was a cavernous place, and the light diminished rapidly as they descended down the deceptively gentle slopes that led them into the interior.

What had happened was that this

land had been subject to many volcanic eruptions hundreds of thousands of years ago. Flint knew, if only a little dimly, about such things. Much of the rock that had been thrown to the surface was a hard-looking limestone, but this was easily eroded by water, and this is what had happened over the years since, while the water from the hills had brought down seeds and soil, giving canyons like this their own unique character, with plants and trees growing freely and branching systems coming off the main body of the formation.

It wasn't hard for them to detect the cows either; a lowing sound from one of the sub-canyons alerted them to the fact that a substantial number of the animals had been herded together in one of these. As they came closer they saw that the way across the entrance had been blocked by a crudely made gate that prevented the animals from surging forwards and taking their fill of the grass that filled the deeper part of the canyon floor.

There was no sign of the rustlers, but Flint had been in such places before, and he knew that the rustlers' instinct would be to find somewhere more secure where they could make their camp.

'Rosie, Travis, you stay behind as defenders while I investigate with Chang,' said Flint.

'If you think . . .' began Rosie hotly in a whisper that was damped down by their surroundings — but Travis gave her a warning look, and she subsided. 'OK, I'll stay with Pops, make sure he keeps out of trouble.'

'Thanks,' said Flint with a wry smile on his face, knowing that in a way Travis was the very protection Rosie needed, rather than the other way about. In the back of his mind was the thought that she had been a good guide to get the two men there, but now she needed to stay behind so the men could get on with the work. He was like most of the men of his generation in that he considered putting a woman in danger the wrong thing to do, even if they themselves were willing to do so.

The vegetation in such canyons tended to be thickest where the water table was the highest, but it looked as if over the past few months the thickest growths had been brought low by scything or with machetes to give the criminals room to move around and do their work.

It turned out that Skeleton Canyon was not straight, either, and that the main area curved around steeply, which was why they had not been spotted straightaway, along with the fact that the walls of the canyon were uneven, sticking out sometimes several feet at a stretch.

They passed another cattle pen and Flint had a swift look inside, which was easy to do because the so-called gate was crudely made, with uneven horizontal strips and several verticals on to which they were lashed, leaving plenty of spaces in between. Flint noticed that many of the cows were mothers with young calves. This was a bonus to the rustlers because it meant that such animals were unbranded and fresh, and would fetch a good price across the border.

He and Chang walked on, but it was that very cattle pen that was to prove their undoing. They heard a sound behind them that they would not have noticed in the outside world and turned, thinking that Rosie might have caught up with them after all — but instead they saw a man beside the crudely made gate who had obviously been in beside the animals, inspecting them for one reason or another.

He was a young cowboy dressed in loose, light clothing, but with a hat on to keep off the many insects that buzzed around — but this was not what drew their attention.

He was holding a 12-bore shotgun and was pointing it at the level of their stomachs, covering both men, and he spent little time in making his wishes known.

'Turn around men, and move on, or you're both dead.'

* * *

Rosie was not pleased at being left behind. In fact she rather resented being a kind of nursemaid for her father, and as she watched Flint and Chang leave she was possessed with a desire to march after them. The insects did not help either, they buzzed constantly through the air and settled on anything or any-one that did not move a great deal. She waved her arms impatiently and she found her father was looking at her with an ironic smile on his face.

'Just can't stop yourself, can you?'

'What?'

'You want to be off and tracking 'em down. Well, you know what, these old legs could do with a stretch, so why don't we do precisely what we shouldn't, and go after those boys and keep 'em out of trouble?'

'So much for protection,' said Rosie.

'You got to promise me that if any fighting starts you'll get out of here,' said her father, losing some of the twinkle in his eyes: 'I couldn't bear it if I lost my girl.' She saw the naked truth in his eyes, and she smiled in a winning manner.

'Pops, you know I've always tried to do my best by you,' but she turned her head so that he did not see the glint in her eyes that indicated she would disobey if she had to. Anyway, she knew she was not fooling him for one minute.

They followed the two at a discreet distance, and they were glad that they did so, for they saw the rustler emerging from where the cattle were penned up. They had seen the second pen before this, and Travis had shaken his head on seeing the calves there.

'This don't make sense,' he said.

'What do you mean?' asked Rosie.

'Rustlers don't operate on this time scale; they want to get in and take as many steers as they can, sell them and make off with a clear profit. When did the first raids happen?'

'I never thought — two, three months ago?'

'Then it really don't make sense.'

Both of them fell silent when the young man appeared, except Travis gave a gasp of recognition. They watched the capture of Chang and Flint, and the march forward around the curve of the canyon.

'Hell,' said Travis, 'it's Brock Pearce, I'd know that little cuss anywhere.'

'So it is,' whispered Rosie, her anger rising.

Brock Pearce had been one of their cattle managers. At first he had been a capable young man who had helped in the first season of transporting cattle to Deming to be shipped on the trains. The trouble was, Pearce had been a bit too fond of the gambling tables and the bright lights of town and had returned late to his duties, although at least he had shipped the cattle efficiently. His tardiness and laziness in leaving jobs to others meant that Travis had eventually let him go.

Rosie raised her gun to shoot down the man who was threatening her companions but Travis pushed it down with a thin hand.

'Easy,' he whispered.

They saw the gunman take the two prisoners, and watched as he began marching them off to wherever the rustlers had their quarters. Seeing how distracted the man was, Travis gave a slight nod and they swiftly followed after. If two of their team were summarily executed it would halve their numbers, and it wouldn't be long before Travis and his daughter were tracked down and killed too. The only reason the intruders had not been killed was because they had not shown any fight. Although he was breaking his own stricture about protecting his own daughter, Travis knew that getting their companions back would protect her in the long run.

'Hands up, mister,' said Rosie, once she was not too far from Pearce. The former manager turned, and it was obvious that he was not about to let some stranger attack him, but the sight of Rosie standing there was enough to cause him to pause for a second or two, a fatal mistake when he had left Flint and Chang unguarded. Too late he realized his error, and raised his rifle to kill Rosie so he could turn back to his former prisoners, but Flint was upon him. Flint didn't even need to shoot, he simply smacked the man on the back of the head with his Colt 45. No one had ever pointed out what a heavy object this particular weapon was, but it had real heft and there was a distinct 'crack' as it caught the man on the back of the head. As Flint stepped back, Chang stepped in, and his fists were a blur again as he punched the man in the lower back, at the point that corresponded with his kidneys.

Pearce gave a grunt of pain and fell face forwards into the foliage through which they had been walking. He was still alive, but breathing in an impressively stentorian manner.

'When he wake up will not be able to walk for long time,' said Chang impassively, but Flint could sense an air of satisfaction in the Chinaman's demeanour.

'Good work,' said Flint, but he glared a little at Rosie, who was just being joined by Travis. 'I thought I told you to stay behind on guard?' his voice was low, but his disapproval was strong. Rosie holstered her guns and stood there hands on her hips, her face becomingly flushed as she stared at him.

'Joe Flint, I was worried, he was going to get you both killed.'

'Yeah, well we were waiting for our chance,' said Flint. 'It ain't the first time I've been on the wrong end of a shotgun. We was going to slow down so that he came close, irritated with us, then Chang was going to do that fast thing and sweep the feet out of under him while I clonked him on the bean, leaving him much the same as this.' Chang gave a swift nod of agreement. 'Still, thanks Rosie,' added Flint casually.

'You're welcome,' said the girl, a little mollified, 'but seeing as you're so high and mighty, next time ten of them can hold you up and I'll just leave you to it.'

Travis looked around expertly. Now that his girl was safe he was studying the lie of the land.

'They won't be far off,' he said. 'They'll want to be fairly close to the entrance of the canyon, but on a spot where they can strike camp on solid ground.'

'Right, well we'll separate again,' said Flint. 'We'll take one side, and you and Rosie take the other.'

Below them the ground underneath the coarse grass was uneven, and undulated in a such a manner that one minute they were walking downwards, and a hundred feet later were walking upwards again. It was lucky for them that the camp, such as it was, lay at the bottom of one of the downward slopes. There was an area of flat rock that stuck out from the side of the canyon like an uneven plate at least fifty feet wide. It was the kind of solid base that was a boon to rustlers like these, who had established their living quarters here. Four canvas 'A'.framed tents, one of them large, were dotted around the base camp. Seating consisted of dry, hollow logs that had been dragged on to the platform. Various items of clothing and weaponry were scattered around, besides the bones of the animals that had been cooked to sustain the gang.

As usual, the fire was the centrepiece of the camp, and this had a spit across the top just like the one they had seen in Mexico, since this was the only practical way to cook meat without burning it badly in the process. The fire itself was low, although from the pile of dry wood at the side of the camp Flint guessed it would be stoked up in the long evenings when the winds soughed over the hills and the coyotes howled in the darkness.

Four men were seated around the fire, and from their attitudes it was clear they had just emerged from their afternoon siesta, secure in the knowledge that they were being guarded in their sleep. Travis and Rosie were much further from the camp than Flint and Chang, who were like two statues as they stood beside an outcrop of rock overlooking their enemy. Flint stole a look across the intervening distance and was perceptive enough to see that Travis had stiffened even more, as if he had become a statue of himself. There was a look on the old man's face that Flint could not interpret, but he suspected it was to do with the fact that he had finally caught up with the criminals who were damaging his business.

Flint decided that it was time to take action. If Travis was motivated by hatred there was no saying what he might do in anger, putting the rest of the party in danger. Flint cursed the fact that the old man was there at all — they should have followed their first instinct and tied him up in a tent.

Flint looked at Chang, and the same thought passed between the two men: they charged the encampment, parting quite a bit as they did so, making sure that they were a harder target to hit than if they stayed close together.

However this was not the only thing that happened, for as they ran, they were immediately noticed by the four men. Chang widened his eyes and opened his mouth showing twin rows of tobacco-stained teeth, and screamed at the top of his voice. It was a disconcerting sight and sound, and it threw the men they were attacking into a state of fear and panic. They ran for their weapons, some of the guns being in belts near their side, and the other two for rifles that were leaning at the side of the hollowed-out logs.

Flint, however, was not one to waste bullets on an enemy. He managed to reach one man who was struggling to free his pistol and punched the man on the chin — hard. The rustler fell to the ground as if he had been hit by a club. Chang ran up to another man and whirled round in the air once more, seeming to rise off the ground with ease, kicking the weapon away from the man. However, his opponent was young and fit, and he managed to jump the log and get away from his attacker. Chang sprang forward in hot pursuit of his enemy — but then there was the click of a rifle being primed, a click that sprang through the damp air of the canyon. Another young man, who was obviously only a few years older than Rosie, was armed and pointing his Remington at the two men.

Flint was a good shot, but he had been attacking one of the other three men, and had unwisely turned his back on the fourth.

'Pull out your guns and drop 'em,' said the young man, 'and you, Mister Slit-eye, give those feet and fists a rest or you're going to be dead meat.' Chang pulled back with a sullen look on his face, and faced the man with the rifle. The man Flint had been tackling took advantage of the pause in hostilities to take Flint's guns out of his hand and holster, and point them at his back.

'Pummel me, would ya?' said the rustler with scorn, and the tone in his voice told Flint that he might be a dead man in the next five minutes.

Things were looking bad for the two men, except for the fact that they knew they were being backed in their attack.

'Put down your rifle,' said Rosie — she was running forward now. The man turned his head and looked at her. The young one on the other side of the log gave a snort of contempt.

'Some girl,' he said.

But the one who was holding the rifle half-turned while still keeping his weapon pointed at Chang.

'Rosie,' he said, but in a tone that did not hold a great deal of surprise.

'Stop this now, Chuck,' said his sister.

17

'Yep, give it up now son,' said Travis coming down the slope towards the camp at a surprising pace, holding his own pistol in his hand and with a hardness to his voice that had not been there before.

'Say, Dad, never thought I'd see you here,' said Charles, his only surviving son. He had turned more fully towards his sister and father. The rustler standing behind Flint saw what was happening, and stepped out from behind the sheriff so that he could train the stolen weapons on the new arrivals.

Chang, noticing that his enemy was distracted, ran forward at a speed that seemed to be almost inhuman. He was at least a foot smaller than Chuck, but his fists went into a blur as he punched the man to the ground and snatched the rifle off him.

Flint was no slouch, either. He knew

how heavy and unwieldy his Colts were in the hands of someone untrained in their use. Now that they were no longer pointing at his kidneys he took a leaf out of Chang's book and chopped viciously at the wrist of the man at his side. The numbing motion made the man drop the gun he held in that hand, and as he swung around to shoot Flint with the gun in his right hand, the sheriff simply moved with him so that he was no longer in the spot being aimed at, and took a vicious side swipe at the man's neck. The rustler gave a choked groan and clutched at his neck with his free hand, the gun pointing downwards in the other.

Flint grabbed the man's right wrist and twisted his arm so that the man was in agony, such agony that he dropped the gun in his right hand, which also clattered to the ground. Flint could not leave his opponent standing: he brought to bear a satisfactory uppercut that felled the man to the ground, and unless he was pretending — which, judging by his bloody nose and hard breathing, he wasn't — then he was out cold.

The one remaining free criminal started running towards the tents in which more weapons would be kept. There was no time for any fancy games such as chasing him. Flint got down on his knees and snatched up one of his Colts, instinct took over and when he fired it was straight at the legs of his enemy. The man gave a wordless scream and keeled over with a rapidly spreading stain on the canvas of his blue jeans.

'You shot me, you bastard, you shot me,' he wailed. Flint could have informed him that he might have been shot but at least it was through the fleshy part of the leg, which meant he might bleed, but at least he would live.

Rosie and her father pulled Chuck to his feet and the young man swayed there like a tree in the wind. While Chang and Flint made sure that the other three men were secured, and in some cases bandaged, they confronted the relative and ringleader.

'How could you have done this?' asked

Travis, a look of agony on his face. 'Why are you trying to destroy me? My own son.'

'Really? You never treated me like a son. You gave me little, you bossed me around, and from a young age you whipped me. I hated you then, and it wasn't some lesson for life where I was gonna forgive you. You brought me to the lowest of the low, and there was no give in you.' Chuck stopped and stared straight into his father's face. Travis was not the kind to flinch or look away, but there was a blue tinge to his lips as he gazed on his errant son.

'You were a wild, undisciplined youth. From your little years you were a rapscallion hell-hound, and your mother, your mother, she didn't help, let you have your way in everything. What was I supposed to do? You were allowed to get away with your wild behaviour until I had to step in.'

'She hated you, too,' said Chuck.

'Who?' asked Travis, in an unbelieving tone.

'Maw, that's who, you put her through all that suffering, all those babies that died. She couldn't stand you near her in the end.'

'Chuck,' said Rosie, 'shut up.' But it was too late: an incoherent sound came from the lips of the old man, and he clutched at his face as if trying to grab something that had settled over his face, his breathing became laboured, then he fell to the ground. For the first time the arrogant sneer that had been covering the features of his only son vanished. Rosie turned her attention to her father, falling to her knees beside the stricken man. Flint and Chang were distracted elsewhere, and Charles Gordon knew the canyon inside out: he said nothing, but threw his body off the rocky platform they had used as a camp site, and fled towards the undergrowth in the lower reaches of the canyon where the plant life and the light were at their worst, where the outcrops of limestone created dark caverns and endless hiding places for a fleeing individual.

Flint had seen what was happening out of the corner of his eye as he was tying one of his captives with some rope they had found amongst the supplies that kept the rustlers going. But by the time he got to his feet Chuck had vanished like snow on a river, and like that snow, a moment white then gone forever.

Flint did the only thing a man could do: he sprang forwards and began to follow the escapee.

Rosie was cradling her father in her arms. His lips were blue.

'My medicine,' he gasped. She fumbled in his jacket pocket and managed to find the bottle of glycerine, which she quickly uncorked and waved under his nose. By this time Flint had fled after her brother. Rosie looked down at her father with tears in her eyes, but Travis looked back at her and just nodded his head slightly. The unspoken message went between them.

'Are you sure?' she asked, and he managed another feeble nod. Rosie gently let him go and stood up with a grim expression on her face. She knew from the unspoken message that she was going after Flint for a reason. Flint was not that bothered about the fact that Chuck was her brother — to him, Chuck was just another criminal who needed to be caught by any means necessary. She did not want to see her sibling being killed, no matter what he had done.

She was built like a particularly curvy greyhound, her legs as long as the man she was pursuing, so it wasn't long before she caught up with Flint.

'Great idea,' he said, 'just be careful, you stay a few feet away from me at the same level and we'll soon take care of him.'

'We'll take care of him all right,' said Rosie, speaking in a voice that showed the fierce matriarch she would become one day if she survived this latest encounter. 'Chuck, come out here this minute, don't you realize what you've done?'

'Hell,' said Flint, 'I guess he knows what he's done all right, that's why he did it!' Shaking his head he chased even deeper into the canyon, but walking rather than running, for the simple reason that he wanted his eyes to become increasingly used to the dimming light. This was one canyon that lived up to its name because it was getting increasingly deep.

They were not helped by the fact that the undergrowth was becoming thicker, and this was obscuring their view as they travelled onwards.

Flint was becoming increasingly irritated as he walked on, because all it needed was for Chuck to steal past them further along and head back to the camp site, which was the main reason he and Rosie were also moving apart from each other.

But she was growing more and more impatient with whatever was going on. She charged forward and shouted at the top of her voice:

'Chuck, this is hellish — think of what we meant to each other, you're killing Pops. He could be dead already for all I know.'

She had come to a sudden clearing where the ground was stonier than in other areas. That was when Chuck, her big brother, stepped out in front of her. In the meantime Flint was circling the undergrowth around the clearing, as stealthy as a big cat knowing that he had to be ready to take his chance.

Chuck stood there with his rifle in his hand.

'Let me go, Rosie,' he said, 'you know what he was like. He was a hard man, he did me down and you knew it.'

'He wanted you to be the best, that's why he was so hard on you.'

'I hated him; it was him that killed my maw.'

'Mother, she was a force of nature. She didn't do anything she didn't want to do. You're just seein' things the way you want to see them. He's no better and no worse than any other rancher — he might be dead.'

'Then I'm done and outta here.' He began to move away from her.

'Stop where you are,' said Rosie her

guns appearing in her hands.

'What are you going to do? Shoot me?' the contempt in his voice was almost palpable. Then suddenly he whirled around and raised his rifle and pointed it at her. 'Don't make me do this.'

She fired on her own brother, tears running down her cheeks as she pulled the triggers of her guns. But just as her fingers were tightening on the triggers a figure came crashing out of the undergrowth and descended like a wolverine on the bigger man, knocking him to the ground while the shots passed harmlessly over their heads.

Joe Flint was used to fighting with his fists. Long before he was a sheriff he had had to survive in work camps where he sometimes had to battle hard to survive. He gave no quarter, and did not give the younger man the chance to recover from the initial rush, his fists pounding the enemy into the ground, breaking one of the other man's ribs in the process.

'You piece of hell-bound scum, you're going where you won't see the day for a long time, and they hang rubbish like you.' He pounded some more, taking out his fury on the young rustler with a ferocity that had a lot to do with how Chuck's depredations on the Gordon homestead and his own relatives had made him feel. But he was prevented from taking out his full anger when he felt a pair of strong but slim hands pulling at his shoulders, and this brought him back to sanity.

He moved back and stood up, his fists still bunched, dark hair spilling over his face, breathing heavily and a look of flushed anger on his normally calm features as he stood over the inert man. It was Rosie, who had dropped her guns and was pulling him away, and they stood over the unconscious man.

'I'm glad I didn't kill my own brother,' said Rosie, as Flint turned and embraced her with a force that showed the real power in his taut body.

18

It was two days later; Flint was coming back into Greenville with his prisoners, helped by Chang and Rosie. He had helped get Travis back to his ranch the previous day. Travis had lost a lot of colour, but he rallied on the way back and his lips were no longer blue, even by the time they got him home. Rosie was taking no chances with her doting parent, and ordered him to go straight to his bed. Travis had protested at this, but he had admitted to his youngest that he was indeed tired, although he would not make a move until he had a quiet word with the sheriff concerning Charles Gordon, who was currently tied up in one of the barns with his henchmen.

When they were alone in his private office Travis looked at Flint with a face that was far whiter than it should have been.

'Don't hang my boy,' he said, 'he and

Rosie are all I have left of Mary. He did it to hurt me, that I'm sure of, but that don't mean he has to die for it.'

'Travis, I've gotten to know you as a real good support,' said Flint. 'You knew fine well what it could mean for us all if we went into Mexico and broke a whole bunch of international treaties, heck it was the reason why I left my deputy, Brent, to look after that bunch of miscreants. I couldn't put him through any more after what he's suffered. You're a good man, in your time you've been a hard man. These two were your youngest, and I guess you didn't spare the rod with the boy. You were hard on him for what you saw as his own good.'

'I guess I was, but that don't explain what you're going to do with him.'

'Rustling's a hangin' offence,' said Flint. 'Them steers are a man's livelihood, and when they're gone it can destroy him, and that's what that man tried to do to you.'

'I guess,' said Travis, 'but if he died because of his revenge on me — well,

I guess that would be another way of bringing me to an end. 'Sides I've had a word with the guys, and one or two of 'em knows Skeleton Canyon and they'll go out there, herd the steers and get 'em back real quick.'

'Well, if there's no loss and you don't want to press charges against him, I guess we could arraign them for lesser charges, temporary loss of property, fighting with the law. Take away the rustling aspect altogether, at your behest, then I guess we could get them for attackin' representatives of the law.' He did not comment on the look of relief that came over the features of the rancher. 'I'll still have to take them in, and they'll do jail time, but at least you and Rosie'll get to see him. Maybe you can build some bridges, maybe not, but at least you'll get some kind of chance to make and mend.'

He was thinking these thoughts as he brought the men in one by one and locked them up with the help of Brent and Chang. Rosie came in just as they were imprisoning her brother.

'Chuck,' was all she said. He looked at her, and although there was a look of defiance, there was no sign of any hatred towards her — indeed he looked faintly ashamed as he sat down on the bed in his cell with a rattle of his manacles.

'He was so old,' said Chuck, 'so different. I thought I wanted to hurt him real bad, but he's hurt bad enough.' He looked at the sheriff: 'How much time will I get, sheriff?'

'If we work it right, maybe a year,' said Flint frankly, 'a year each for you and your men.'

'They're good boys,' said Chuck. 'They were paid out of my savings. They'll do well on the outside; none of them ever stole a dime before.'

'Keep it for the circuit judge,' said Brent, clanging the door on the last prisoner. 'I think he's in town in the next fortnight.'

'Be good to get the office back,' said Flint, referring to the Mexicans, Dexter and Duke, all of whom were still incarcerated in the building. 'Place is getting a little crowded.'

'Come with me,' he went outside with Rosie and Chang. 'Thank you for your help, Chang, I will personally see to it that the state rewards you for your efforts.' Chang gave a faint bow.

'You are welcome, Flint, wise sheriff, you show the right amount of wisdom, but these were angry men, they were not killers. Now they be punished, but not lose their lives. For the money, I will use any to help my sons get lessons and learn more.' He bowed more deeply to them both. 'Now I return and do my real work. It has been an exciting time. Adventure was mine. I'll see my boy now,' his normally expressionless face split into a mischievous grin, and he departed for his home and family.

Flint was left facing Rosie, the both of them silent now, and he was aware that she was looking at him in a way he had feared.

'Thanks Sheriff Flint — Joe —' she said, then came forward and kissed him full on the lips. He pulled back after a few seconds and held her at arms' length.

'Rosie, that ain't the way. Once the trial's over you'll return to your own life and you'll marry some nice young cattle man. You'll run the business as good as any man.'

'Joe!' they were aware of a figure that turned the corner, coming rapidly towards them. It was Katie-Jo, and her upright form and long legs propelled her forwards rapidly to where they both were. She was not a woman to show her emotions in public, but she grabbed hold of Flint and held him for long enough to show her feelings. 'I heard you were back, I just had to come and see you. Don't go into the wilds again!' she scolded him as if he was one of her naughty children, and then hugged him again. Flint looked at Rosie, who had stepped backwards, a faintly stricken look on her pretty face.

'I'll get Brent to take you home,' he said. 'Look after your father, Rosie — and get to know Brent — he's a special guy. It's been a strange time, but I'm real glad we got to know each other.' He held out his hand, and she shook it as vigorously as most men he knew, and this time the smile that lit up her face was real.

* * *

It was nearly two months later. The bank and loan had prospered along with the area. Travis Gordon and his daughter had given evidence at the trial of the men who had stolen their cattle, along with his son, and with his special pleading their sentences had been limited to just over a year each.

Duke had been sentenced too, for his part in the desert robbery, but it was rapidly decided that Judd had been the brains of the outfit — if indeed any part of the brain had been used in the process — and he was imprisoned for a period of ten years, but he would still be a fairly young man when released, and still had time to change his life.

Dexter was hanged for what he had done with his *vaqueros*, and showed no remorse as he was led to the gallows. His men were imprisoned for their part in the plot, and when they were released they would be deported to Mexico.

Brent hit it off with Rosie on the way back to the Gordon ranch so well that he spent more and more of his spare time riding between that place and Greenville to see the woman who rapidly became the biggest part of his life.

As ever, when it came to Flint, Katie-Jo could not make up her mind yet to marry the man she loved, but peace seemed to descend on the town, and he decided that he would ask her one more time once the Greenville Raiders were a distant memory and there was no more conflict.

He was walking along the main street thinking about this very thing when three people appeared: a man, a woman and a little girl.

'Sheriff Flint!' shouted the little girl, her jaw having healed since the last time he had seen her, and ran towards him.

'Lindy,' said Flint, grabbing her and swinging her off the ground and through the air, setting her down as she gave a squeal of surprise and pleasure. 'Great, you're all better now, you'll never stop talking, wee one.'

Ben stuck out his bear-like hand and engulfed the sheriff's in a firm handshake, while his wife, Lindy senior, smiled beside him.

'You did a great thing, Flint,' said Ben.

'Yes, you did,' said his wife, putting her arm around Lindy as the girl came to her side.

'Bad men all gone,' said Lindy, 'you got them, didn't you Sheriff?'

'I sure did,' said Flint, and he winked at the girl and smiled at Ben.

'Lindy's going to school again, and she's got all her friends, and we never talk about any of the bad stuff,' said Ben. 'And now I sell ice cream in the store and I let her help me when she's finished school.'

'Ben, you're a wise man,' said Flint.

'Sheriff, you're another,' and Flint watched as the contented family walked away together under the midday sun.

Other titles in the
Linford Western Library:

KEE-TO, IRON HAND

Art Isberg

Kee-To, Iron Hand is the one Sioux leader white soldiers have never been able to corner or capture. His daring raids and uncanny ability to avoid being behind bars have made him a priority for the cavalry officers to find and jail. But Kee-To has the blood of his fighting ancestors, and their mystical whispers to him, to keep him free. He would rather die than let the horse soldiers pen up his people behind fences under guard. A battle is looming as the Sioux prepare to journey to the safety of Canada. Can Kee-To prevail one last time?